TEXTUAL
Relations

USA Today and International Bestselling Author
Lauren Rowe

Copyright © 2023 by Lauren Rowe

All rights reserved.

No part of this book may be reproduced in any form or by any electronic or mechanical means, including information storage and retrieval systems, without written permission from the author, except for the use of brief quotations in a book review.

Published by SoCoRo Publishing

Cover design © Letitia Hasser, RBA Designs

1
GRAYSON

Oh, God, no. Not this again.

That's what I think as I sit on my bed and read the disheartening text that just landed on my phone.

> Sorry, Grayson. I'm not Katie. Double-check the number she gave you. If you entered it correctly, then it appears she didn't "thoroughly enjoy" last night's "stimulating conversation" at Captain's as much as you did.

Shit.

Why do women keep giving me fake numbers in bars after what I thought was a great conversation? It's particularly baffling to me that it could keep happening at Captain's weekly Singles Night, where everyone ostensibly came for the same reason: to meet other singles.

I know I'm not a "lady killer" sort of guy. I'm shy and on the nerdy side. Plus, I don't get to the gym nearly as often as I should. But if a woman's not digging me, then why not say so in the moment, rather than laughing at my jokes and replying "sure thing!" after I've mustered the nerve to ask for her number?

If a woman told me to my face she wasn't feeling it, then I'd be able to ask her *why*. What better way to improve my flirting game than collecting real-time data from a member of my target demographic? I'd be able to turn rejections into focus groups!

Surely, it'd sting in the moment to hear a woman tell me, in brutal detail, all the reasons she's not attracted to me. But I'd prefer that brief infliction of pain to leaving the bar with a spring in my step and a fake number in my pocket, only to find out later the woman who smiled and laughed was actually plotting her escape the whole time. Is getting a free cocktail really worth humiliating someone?

Without honest feedback, I've got no idea what I'm doing wrong. Is it that I come off as too eager and should slow my roll? Do I need to stop telling women the unglamorous truth about what I do for a living—namely, that I work in the IT department at a law firm—but, instead, tell them I'm something cool, like a racecar driver or audiobook narrator? Or is the problem something unfixable, like my face?

Tipsy women often tell me I've got an "adorable" face—a "baby face" they want to pinch, poke, and prod, often while cooing at me like I'm a six-foot puppy. Unfortunately, though, after having their way with my cheeks and dimples, women tend to leave the bar with someone else. Usually, a dude with smooth pick-up lines and confidence oozing out his pores. Guys like my buddy from work, an attorney named Max. He not only has a lucrative job to go with his bad-boy good looks, he's perfected the art of making women chase *him*. Mostly, it seems to me, by acting like an arrogant jerk who doesn't give a shit. And that's just not me. Never has been, never will be.

A car honks its horn outside my bedroom window, drawing me from my wandering thoughts. With a deep sigh, I return to my phone and tap out a reply to the actual owner of Katie's fake number.

> Me: Thanks for the reply. I definitely texted the right wrong number. Katie entered her number into my phone, and I clicked on it when sending my text. Womp.

Unknown: Aw, that's a bummer, Grayson. Chin up, though. There's always next time.

> Me: That's the way the ball bounces. It wasn't the first time and probably won't be the last I get a fake number in a bar. It's rough out there.

Unknown: How many times has this happened to you?

> Me: This is the third fake number in about two months. In defense of the women, though, I'm terrible at flirting. I was in a long-term relationship that ended about six months ago, and it seems I've got a lot to improve upon in my flirting game.

Unknown: Practice makes perfect! A few more rounds in the ring, and you'll be back in fighting form in no time.

> Me: That assumes I was in "fighting form" at some earlier date, when in fact, I've always been lame at flirting.

Unknown: LOL. I'm sure you're not nearly as lame as you think. Let's look at the math. How many real phone numbers have you gotten in the same two-month period? In baseball, a batting average of .300 is considered fantastic.

> Me: Sadly, it's been Goose Egg City for me since my relationship ended. The good news, though, if we're going to use baseball metaphors, is I haven't been "up to bat" all that many times. I only started stepping up to the plate in earnest two months ago, after discovering weekly Singles Night at Captain's. It's much less daunting for a shy person like me to try "swinging my bat" when I know everyone at the bar is single and open to at least chatting.

> Unknown: I love Captain's. Best martinis in town! I've never been on Singles Night, though. Is it every Thursday night?

> Me: Yeah, at least at their Seattle location. I don't know about their other ones.

I've already been thinking this mystery person is a woman, based on the tone of the conversation. And she's presumably single, too, given her interest in Singles Night at Captain's. And so, with that profiling in mind, my latest message is my way of trying to confirm that this presumably single woman is located in Seattle, like me. I'm assuming she is, based on the area code of her phone number. But with the transportability of cell phones, you never know if someone resides where their number would suggest.

> Unknown: I'm in Seattle. Wouldn't it be a funny coincidence if we got to talking one night at Captain's and both suddenly realized we'd already had this text conversation?

Well, it wouldn't be a funny coincidence if we made a date to meet, I think. But that thought is immediately followed by, *Calm the fuck down, Grayson. You don't even know for sure if this person is a woman. And even if she is, you have no idea what she looks like or how old she might be.*

I tap out the question "What's your name?" But quickly delete it without pressing Send. If this third fake phone number has taught me anything, it's that coming across as too friendly and eager is a turn-off to women. Obviously, I need to take a chill pill.

On the other hand, though, I'd hate to wonder "what if." If I don't shoot my shot with this mystery person, how will I ever know if the ball would have gone into the net? I begin typing my reply, deciding to try to nudge the conversation in the right direction, while still, hopefully, not coming across as too eager:

> Me: Yeah, that'd be funny. If ever I bump into you there, I'd want to buy you a drink to thank you for taking so much of your valuable time to give me a pep talk.

> Unknown: No need to thank me. I'm enjoying talking to you! You're obviously a sweetheart, which I'd already surmised from your darling text to Katie. It's her loss, Grayson. And as far as me taking my "valuable time" to talk to you, I waited until I was doing nothing but relaxing in a bathtub with a big glass of Chardonnay to text you back. Sorry if waiting all day to get a response to your dinner invitation was stressful for you. I would have texted sooner, but I had a hectic day at work.

Okay, that settles it. *She's a woman.* Because a dude wouldn't be taking a bath, for one thing, and especially not with a glass of white wine. Also, a dude wouldn't have called me a "sweetheart" and said my text to Katie was "darling" and that missing out on me was "Katie's loss." Plus, there's no way in *hell* any man would even think to apologize for not responding to me sooner.

Hot damn! Now I *really* want to know more about this mystery woman. How old is she? What does she look like? And most importantly, assuming she's within striking distance of my age, is she game to get out of that bathtub right now and meet me at Captain's for one of their renowned martinis?

> Me: I'm enjoying talking to you, too. And no worries about your delay in replying. I'm grateful you replied at all.

> Unknown: If you don't mind me asking, how long were you with your girlfriend?

> Me: Five years.

> Unknown: That's a long relationship. How old are you?

> Me: 25.

> Unknown: Well, shit, that explains everything! You might be 25, but you're more like 20, in terms of your experience with flirting and dating. No wonder you've still got a bit to learn. You've only been practicing on one woman for the past five years. And those were some particularly formative years for you.

> Me: That's an excellent point.

Unknown: Just keep putting yourself out there, and I promise you'll get more and more confident with flirting, which in turn will make you more and more attractive to women. If there's one thing women find irresistible, it's confidence. Confidence turns an attractive person into an irresistible one.

Me: That explains why my buddy is so successful with women. Whenever we go out, he acts like an arrogant, cocky jerk to women, and they practically line up to go home with him.

Unknown: Good lord. Do NOT emulate that strategy, unless, of course, you're only looking for casual sex with 20-somethings. No judgment, if you are, but that's not the vibe I got from your text to Katie. If you're looking for an actual relationship, as I suspect, then aim to radiate confidence, but not cockiness. And always treat women with respect.

Me: Oh, I'd never treat any woman disrespectfully. And, yes, you've deduced accurately I'm looking for a girlfriend. Obviously, I'd very much like to get laid by said girlfriend, frequently. But I'm a one-woman kind of guy.

Unknown: You're so sweet and funny! And, yes, I never doubted you want to get laid. That's to be expected for a young buck of 25. You're in the thick of your sexual prime.

Me: God, I hope not, or else I'm wasting precious time. Since my break-up, my dating life has been more PainHub than PornHub.

Unknown: LOL. If you don't mind me asking, who broke up with whom in your relationship? If your girlfriend broke up with you, did she tell you why? That would be helpful for me to know, seeing as how I'm now dispensing dating advice to you.

Me: I'm the one who broke up with her, but only AFTER finding out she'd been cheating on me for six months. So, in a way, she broke up with me first, without me realizing it.

Unknown: Ugh. Been there, done that. My ex-husband cheated on me, too, and for a lot longer than six months.

Me: Ugh. For how long?

Unknown: Four years that I know of. Probably a lot longer, but that's as far back as our phone records went.

Me: Asshole! I'm sorry you had to go through that.

Unknown: Thanks. I was devastated when I found out, because I'd given my all to that marriage. But time and therapy have helped me realize he cheated because of his own fragile ego, not because of something I did or didn't do. My ex is a text-book narcissist who needed the ego boost he got from fucking lots of women, many of them your age and younger (!). Plus, I think he got off on all the sneaking around. I've come to realize his cheating had very little to do with me, the same way your ex's cheating almost certainly had very little to do with you.

Me: That's helpful to hear. I was pretty devastated when I found out what she'd been doing. In my case, she only cheated with one guy the whole time, but the texts I found made it clear the sneaking around was part of the fun for her, too.

Unknown: Yup. I don't know how anyone could sneak around like that. I'd never be able to pull it off. I'd feel physically sick all the time.

Me: SAME! I'm the worst liar ever. I can't even play poker.

> Unknown: You're the cutest! I promise if you get back out there and keep your heart open, someone out there will snap you right up.

Oh my God. She's incredible. I have to know more about her. Clearly, she's older than me, based on several things she's said and her general vibe. *But how much older?*

> Me: Is that what you did after your divorce? You got back out there and kept your heart open?

> Unknown: Yes and no. I got back out there, yes, but I'm not looking for a relationship, like you are. I'm happily single by choice these days.

> Me: Does that mean you date, but only casually?

> Unknown: Correct. I go out on dates, now and again, simply because it's fun to flirt and talk to someone new. Plus, I love sex, and a battery-operated boyfriend can only take a girl so far. But I have no desire to make any kind of commitment. I love my life, exactly as is.

Holy fucking shit! She's a goddess! If my skin felt like it was buzzing before, it now feels like it's on fire. She threw out that thing about loving sex so easily—with zero shame or self-consciousness! Talk about a stark one-eighty from Audrey, who blushed and practically curled into the fetal position, every time I begged to give her oral.

> Me: Glad to hear you're living your best life. Would you be willing to be my Hot Teacher and give me some tips on how to improve my flirting skills? I could use a woman's perspective.
>
> Unknown: Hot Teacher, lol. Yes, I'd be happy to try to help you. But I'm quite a bit older than you, so you should take my advice with a grain of salt, assuming you're trying to attract women around your own age.

Before typing my next text, I save her number into my contacts under the name Hot Teacher, just because I find the moniker amusing and sexy.

> Me: I'm open in terms of age. How old are you, if you don't mind me asking?
>
> Hot Teacher: I do mind. First tip, my little Grasshopper, NEVER ask an older woman her age.
>
> Me: Aaaah! Sorry!
>
> Hot Teacher: Rookie error.
>
> Me: I know! I was trying to figure out how many grains of salt I should apply to your advice. I'm thinking the grains of salt to be applied would increase, depending on whether you're old enough to be my mother, grandmother, or great-grandmother. I'm sorry if it was a rude question.

> Hot Teacher: Your reason for asking my age is a good one, so I'll answer you this way: I'm not old enough to be your mother. More like your big sister, like if my parents got divorced and my father went on to remarry your mom and have you. Btw, I don't think you could be rude, if you tried, Grasshopper.

Interesting.

Sounds like she's saying she's anywhere from five to fifteen years older than me. Which means she's most likely in her mid-thirties to early forties, at the most. Which therefore means she's definitely within striking distance, as far as I'm concerned. Men in their forties date women in their twenties, all the time. So, why not the other way around?

> Me: That's helpful to know. Thanks, Hot Teacher! Do you really think women around my age are significantly different from women your age, in terms of what they're looking for in a man?

Hot Teacher: Quite frequently, yes. My single friends and I LOVE when a man is honest and kind and doesn't play games. At our age, we've already chased too many bad boys and womanizers who ultimately weren't worth the effort. But over time, we've realized we did that stupid stuff because we were seeking external validation. These days, we know our worth. If a man can't contribute significantly to the awesome life we've worked hard to create for ourselves, then we don't need or want him! On the other hand, when it comes to younger women like Katie and your ex-girlfriend, they're often still in the phase of this journey called womanhood, in which they're still chasing external validation and the thrill of "capturing" a man who's a walking red flag. Which means they tend to overlook a guy like you who doesn't play games.

Me: Well, shit, based on that explanation, it sounds like a no-brainer for me to date older women.

Hot Teacher: Down, boy. Why don't you try playing the field for a bit with women your own age? Maybe even try acting like a cocky douchebag at a bar, now and again, to get some different kinds of experiences under your belt?

Me: Honestly, even if I could pull off acting like a cocky douchebag (not sure I could), I don't think the women I'd attract would give me the kinds of "experiences" I'd want. I'm looking for a real connection with someone, so why waste time on bullshit?

Hot Teacher: OMG, YOU'RE SO SWEET!

Me: I'm not quite as sweet as you think. I LOVE sex as much as any cocky douchebag, and jacking the beanstalk every night is getting VERY old. It's just that I'd prefer having sex with someone I care about every night to having it with a different, random woman, now and again. When you look at my motivations that way, I'm not being all that sweet, really.

Hot Teacher: You're still sweet. Okay, so maybe you should try meeting women in places other than bars, to avoid the whole meat market thing. Why not try flirting at the grocery store or the dog park, if you have a dog?

Me: Sadly, I don't have a dog. I hope to get one soon. And places like grocery stores are daunting to me in terms of striking up conversations, because everyone always looks so damned busy. Plus, I can't tell who's single.

Hot Teacher: Okay, how about dating apps?

Me: Ugh. Not my strong suit. I rarely get a match, probably thanks to my lame photos, and when I do, I find it hard to keep the conversation going via messages. As I'm sure you've surmised from my rambling text to Katie, I'm not adept at firing off short, pithy texts that keep women coming back for more.

Hot Teacher: LOL. You're keeping me coming back for more pretty damned well. And fuck Katie! That girl wouldn't know a quality man if he bit her in the ass! Actually, that's an excellent segue for another great tip for you, Grasshopper. Grayson-hopper? There's nothing hotter than a man giving his woman a little nibble on her ass cheek when things are getting really spicy. Nothing too aggressive, mind you. I'm talking about a little nibble that lets her know she's so sexy and delicious, you can't contain yourself, not a bite that's deep enough to break her skin. I know you're shy, which I find endearing, but don't be shy in bed. Women love it when a man takes control and goes for it, no holds barred.

. . .

Jesus Christ, I'm hard as a rock.

She *had* to know her message would turn my cock into granite, right? Is that exactly what my naked Hot Teacher in a bathtub specifically intended? And if so, does that mean she's starting to feel sexually attracted to me? Or is this eye-popping text merely a sign she's become tipsy and horny in that warm water, and any anonymous guy would do in this moment?

> Me: Wow, that's one hell of a hot tip, Hot Teacher. I'll definitely keep it in mind the next time I'm fortunate enough to have a bare ass in my face.

> Hot Teacher: Would you be willing to send me a selfie? For research purposes, of course. I want to see what we're working with here, so I can give you the best possible advice.

Aw, fuck.

This is a good news bad news situation. On the one hand, it can't be a coincidence she's only asked for my photo *now*, after our conversation took such a decidedly sexual turn. Doesn't this confirm she's at least slightly curious about me now? That's good news.

On the bad news front, though, I've been enjoying my anonymity with this sexy stranger. In fact, I'm sure I wouldn't have said half the shit I have, if it felt like she was staring into my eyes throughout the entire conversation. What if she sees my baby face and decides she isn't physically attracted to me? What if she feels like she wants to pinch my cheeks and poke at my dimples, the way so many women have done, but doesn't feel the urge to pinch or poke anything else?

Fuck!

But what choice do I have, really? If I balk, she'll assume the worst—that I'm unwilling to send a selfie because I think I'm hideously ugly—which I don't—and that assumption would kill any chance I might have of meeting up with her, regardless.

> Me: Yeah, sure. You want a photo of me smiling? Smoldering? A mugshot?

> Hot Teacher: All of the above. To be clear, this is not a request for a dick pic, Grayson.

> Me: Didn't think it was. Photos coming up.

With my pulse pounding in my ears, I snap all three requested selfies from different angles and send them off, before sitting and waiting for what feels like an eternity for her reply. Intellectually, I know her delay is probably due to my three photos taking a while to download on her end. Emotionally, however, I can't help wondering if she's staring at my face and thinking, "Well, that explains Katie giving him a fake number." Finally, though, when Hot Teacher's text lands on my screen, it's even better than I'd allowed myself to hope for.

> Hot Teacher: OMFG! You're a smoke show, Grayson-hopper! A snack and a half! Look at those beautiful green eyes! Those cute dimples! Those perfect teeth and dark lashes! Stupid Katie! Stupid ex-girlfriend! They're fools!

Feeling like I'm about to keel over from excitement, I type out a reply that says, "Your turn now!" But quickly delete it before sending. There's no doubt in my mind she'd say no to sending me a photo. So, why embarrass myself by asking?

> Me: Thank you! The facial hair is new for me. You think it looks good or should I go back to being clean-shaven?

> Hot Teacher: Don't change a thing! You're perfection! I swear, if I dated younger men, and if you were looking for nothing but a good time, then I'd be VERY tempted to give you some white-hot tips in person, if you know what I mean.

Okay, that's it. I can't hold back a second longer. I have to shoot my shot with this woman, right here and now, or I'll never fucking forgive myself.

> Me: Well, shit, Hot Teacher, let's do it! Meet me for a drink tonight and let's see if our amazing chemistry is still blazing hot in person!

> Hot Teacher: You've never even seen me.

> Me: Hence, the reason I've asked you to meet me for a drink, in person.

> Hot Teacher: Down, boy. What I said was "if" I dated younger men, which I don't. And "if" you were looking for some casual fun, which you're not.

TEXTUAL RELATIONS

> Me: Okay, then, we wouldn't call it a date. Let me buy you a drink to thank you for hyping me up and giving me such great advice.

Hot Teacher: Look at you go! And you claimed to be bad at flirting.

> Me: Does 8:00 at Captain's sound good?

Hot Teacher: I'm tempted. But I don't think so, honey.

> Me: Let's look at this logically. I've surmised our age gap is 5-15 years. Correct?

Hot Teacher: Yes, it's in that range.

> Me: Okay, then our age gap is totally irrelevant. "Stacy's Mom" wasn't a massive hit in a vacuum. The song was such a huge hit because getting with an older woman is a HUGE fantasy for most guys. (Google the song if you don't know it.)

Hot Teacher: I know the song, and I'm certain older women with fantasies of their own had a lot to do with it becoming a smash hit. But even putting our ages aside, there are additional reasons for me to say no, including the fact that you're looking for a girlfriend, and honey, that's not me.

> Me: Okay, I concede I WAS looking for a girlfriend at the beginning of this conversation, but your sage advice has made me realize there's no rush for me to settle down again. I'm only 25 and in my sexual prime, like you said. So why not get out there and bite some asses, maybe even beginning with yours, before looking for my next girlfriend?

Hot Teacher: LOOK AT MY LITTLE GRAYSON-HOPPER GO!

> Me: The bottom line, Hot Teacher, is that I'm highly curious to meet the incredibly sexy, easy-to-talk-to, confident woman who somehow managed to make me feel STOKED I got a fake number last night. At the very least, let me buy you a drink to thank you for bringing such an enormous smile to my face (and even more enormous boner to my pants).

I press send and instantly want to take it back. Why the fuck did I add that last thing about my boner? And even worse, why'd I call it "enormous?" Now, if by some miracle she actually says yes to meeting me, and then lets me bite her ass, she's going to have the highest of expectations about what's hiding behind my pants! How would that be a good thing for me?

Okay, calm down, Grayson. It's the truth, right? You've got a massive boner, literally and figuratively, for this woman, the likes of which you've never felt before. So, why not admit that to her, especially given what she said about sexual confidence being highly attractive? Plus, she's the one who initially broke the seal on dirty talk by saying that thing about ass-biting in the first place. *So, cool your jets.*

The truth is, this mystery woman makes me feel like I can say whatever the fuck I'm honestly thinking, and she'll either encourage me, or tell me "Down, boy." But she won't hold it against me. I don't know why I've suddenly morphed into a swaggering, Max-like lady killer with this stranger, but, damn, I feel high from the unbridled confidence she's pulling out of me just this fast.

> Hot Teacher: *sits up in tub and literally slow claps* That entire text was fucking amazing, Grayson! Sexy, confident, and funny. ALMOST made you utterly irresistible to me! Sadly, however, as mentioned, there are reasons for me to say no to meeting you tonight, in addition to my qualms about our age gap.

> Me: Tell me all the reasons, so I can knock 'em down, one by one.

> Hot Teacher: 1. For all I know, you could be an axe murderer. 2. I've already got plans to have dinner with my girlfriends tonight.

> Me: Only two reasons? Pfft. 1. Every guy you encounter, whether in person or via a wrong-number text, could turn out to be an axe murderer. I'd argue I'm far less likely to be an axe murderer than some other random guy, based on me sending you those photos. If I was planning to chop you up, would I have sent them to you? No way! Especially not the mugshot, which would prove awfully convenient for police during their eventual investigation. 2. Captain's closes at two, so there's plenty of time to meet me AFTER your dinner with friends. Or, hell, since this wouldn't be a date, bring them along with you for after-dinner drinks. All drinks for you and your friends are on me tonight!

> Hot Teacher: Good lord, you're persuasive! But I'm sorry, upon reflection, I can't look past the age gap thing. It'd be too weird for me to mess around with a guy who's not old enough to have fathered my 13-year-old.

Whoa.

Hot Teacher's got a thirteen-year-old kid?

That information momentarily throws me for a loop. But quickly, I'm able to shake it off and realize the revelation doesn't change a damned thing. Of course, she does! She's probably in her late thirties or so, if my hunch is correct. Maybe even her early forties. Plus, she's divorced. So, it makes sense for her to have a kid around that age. In fact, when I think about it, I realize it'd probably be easier to date a woman with a 13-year-old than one with an infant or toddler. Hell, it might even be fun.

> Me: Are you looking for a new daddy for your kid?

> Hot Teacher: Abso-fucking-lutely not.

> Me: Then it's a non-issue, as long as we're both adults. Which we are.

I hold my breath as three dots wiggle underneath my most recent text . . . and then disappear. Fuck! I quickly tap out a message, determined to stave off any kind of definitive rejection from her before she makes a firm decision.

> Me: There's no need for you to decide right now. How about this? I'll go to Captain's tonight around 8:00 and stay put until a) you show up and say hello, or b) the place shuts down and kicks me out. Either way, I'll be there tonight, and the ball will be in your court.

> Hot Teacher: That sounds good. I'd better get ready for dinner with my friends now. I've had fun talking to you.

> Me: I've had fun talking to you, too. Have a great time with your friends. I hope to meet you later. But if not, thanks for turning something embarrassing into something incredible.

> Hot Teacher: The pleasure's been all mine, Grayson.

She attaches a blowing-kiss emoji to the end of her message, which I return in kind. She replies with a basketball emoji, clearly referencing my comment that the ball is in her court, so I respond with a net emoji and praying hands, letting her know I'm praying she'll dunk the ball. And that's how our boner- and smile-inducing conversation finally comes to an end. Hot Teacher doesn't send another message, so neither do I, even though every molecule in my body wants to send her another *ten* texts explaining why our age gap is absolutely meaningless.

I stare at my phone for an eternal moment, just in case Hot Teacher surprises me at the eleventh hour with another text. But when it's clear our conversation is truly over, I force myself to toss my phone onto my nightstand and scream into the void of my ceiling, "Please, God, make her show up!"

I've *never* felt this much chemistry with any woman in my life. Not in person. Not on a dating app. Not even with Audrey, my girlfriend of five fucking years! And certainly not with a woman who'd received the embarrassingly long, rambling dinner invitation I'd stupidly sent to a woman who'd actually wanted nothing to do with me.

I get up and pace my bedroom, feeling too electrified to sit still. What should I wear to the bar? Should I call Max to go with me to Captain's—my buddy from work who always comes with me on Singles Night? I wouldn't invite Max on an actual date, of course, but if Hot Teacher shows up tonight, it'll likely be with a bunch of her friends. So, shouldn't I have at least one friend with me, too, so I don't seem like an overly eager, friendless loser?

"Fuck!" I shout toward the emptiness of my small bedroom,

before grabbing my phone off the nightstand again. My heart pounding, I pull up "Stacy's Mom" and get it cranking. And then, as the campy song blares, I head into my bathroom, hop into the shower, and jerk myself off, all the while fantasizing about a confident, sexy older woman in a bathtub—a smoking hot MILF I've never laid eyes on, but who's already managed to rock my fucking world.

2

GRAYSON

A little before eight, I stride through the front door at Captain's and stop to look around. I've never been here on a Friday night, and it's bumping!

After surveying the packed room, I don't spot Max, who said he'd arrive around eight. But more importantly, I don't see anyone who strikes me as a likely candidate to be Hot Teacher.

I turn around and take two steps toward the bar behind me, figuring I'll grab a drink while I wait for Max, and that's when I see a woman who stops me dead in my tracks.

That's got to be her.

At least, I hope it is.

The woman commanding my full attention seems to be in her late thirties. If she's older than that, she wears it well. As she sits poised at the end of the packed bar, she's ordering from the bartender—smiling and talking to him with the kind of sensual, easy confidence I've been imagining Hot Teacher wears like a magic cloak.

She has shoulder-length, raven hair, high cheekbones, and dark eyes. She's wearing a clingy, red dress that shows off the shape of her ample curves without baring much flesh. She doesn't have a tightly cinched waist and flat belly to go along with her generous bust and round hips, like so many women featured in ads and entertainment. On the contrary, everything about this woman is voluptuous—which I find incredibly sexy. Even more so, because her body language makes it clear she's exceedingly comfortable with her every curve.

I'm sure I'd find this woman physically attractive, even if she came across as shy and unsure of herself. But as it is, her evident comfort in her skin makes her even more compelling to me, providing "proof of concept" of what Hot Teacher said about confidence turning an attractive person into an irresistible one.

As my heart pounds, I continue watching the woman as she accepts her drink—some sort of martini, based on the shape of its glass. I remember Hot Teacher saying Captain's has the best martinis in town. So, did this brunette order a martini to out herself to me . . . or am I assigning meaning to a simple coincidence as a result of wishful thinking?

With my pulse beating in my ears, I watch the woman take a long sip of her drink and say something to the bartender that makes him smile. They chat briefly, until he walks away to serve another customer, at which point the brunette nonchalantly checks her phone.

I shift my weight while continuing to brazenly stare. If that brunette were Hot Teacher, wouldn't she scan the bar looking for me rather than looking at her phone? But I've no sooner had the thought than the woman looks up and begins surveying the packed bar.

Closer and closer, the woman's dark gaze drifts toward me until finally landing on my face . . . and then staying put. *Hello.* When our eyes lock, I feel an insane jolt of adrenaline shooting through me, a tidal wave of energy that sends electricity shooting across my skin and causes a massive, dopey grin to involuntarily unfurl across my face.

She doesn't react to my puppy-dog smile but instead turns her head and nonchalantly takes a dainty sip of her martini. Oh, come on, sweetheart. Must we play games? Surely, a random woman on the receiving end of a smile that big and goofy would react in *some* way, if only to look at the customer next to her to discern if my greeting was perhaps aimed at them. At the very least, a random woman would return my smile, if only half-heartedly, or flash me a "Not a chance, buddy!" look, since it's beyond obvious this goddess is out of my league.

But nope. In the face of my over-the-top grin, this particular woman didn't do any of the things I'd expect but instead chose to do something unnatural. *Nothing.* Which strongly suggests she's Hot Teacher and for some reason doesn't want me knowing that yet.

I continue staring at her profile, willing her to look at me and confirm what my gut already knows. But no dice. For a full two minutes, she continues sipping her martini while glancing anywhere and everywhere but toward me.

"Grayson!" a male voice says. A second later, I feel a nudge on my shoulder.

I peel my eyes off the curvy goddess at the bar and discover my work buddy, Max, standing before me.

Shit.

Instantly, I regret inviting Max to join me tonight. When I texted him, I figured it'd calm my nerves to have a buddy with me in case Hot Teacher showed up with friends. Or, if she didn't show up, I thought it'd be nice to have some company while I drank myself into oblivion until closing time. But now that Max is here, standing mere feet away from the hot brunette I'm dead-ass sure is Hot Teacher, I realize it was pure stupidity to invite him.

What if Hot Teacher decides she likes Max better than me? Max is thirty after all, which is old enough, if only barely, to be her thirteen-year-old's father. Also, Max is a corporate lawyer making six figures, not some lowly IT minion who spends his days exorcising malware from lawyers' laptops. And worst of all, Max has the kind of bad-boy good looks and swagger women can't resist.

Thankfully, I didn't tell Max about the Hot Teacher situation when I texted him earlier, or he'd probably flirt with that brunette simply because he's a competitive guy who'd enjoy showing a newbie like me how it's done.

"Find us a table while I grab us some drinks," Max commands. That's what we usually do when we go out together since Max makes a shit-ton more money than I do.

But this time, as grateful as I am for Max's generosity, there's no way I'm letting him anywhere near the bar. Not when that curvy, charismatic goddess is sitting at the far end of it, and I'm almost positive she's the woman I came here to meet.

"Nah, drinks are on me this time," I say, grabbing Max's arm to stop his movement.

We go back and forth for a bit but ultimately agree I'll buy the drinks while Max finds a table. As Max disappears into the packed crowd, I turn around, eager to make my way toward the brunette. But after only a couple steps, a rowdy group of young women appears in front of me and blocks my progress.

"Excuse me, ladies," I say. "Coming through."

Rather than stepping aside, one of the women grabs my arm like I'm her long-lost friend and shouts, "We're celebrating my bestie's twenty-first birthday!" She indicates another woman in the group—a pretty blonde wearing a sash that reads, "I'm 21 & Hot! Buy me a shot!"—and yells above the din, "Will you buy her a shot?"

"Uh, sure," I reply, partly out of politeness and partly because saying yes seems like the easiest way for me to get past this roadblock. "Do all of you want shots? I'm headed to the bar to place an order, anyway."

The women cheer and thank me profusely—and then quickly

part like the Red Sea to let me pass, now that I'm doing their bidding.

At the bar, I tell myself not to smile at the brunette this time, but instead try to smolder the way Max always does . . . But shit! When I glance down the length of the bar, the hot brunette isn't there anymore.

I turn around and scan the place, my heart racing, and, to my relief, discover the curvy brunette walking with a group of women around her age toward the back of the bar.

I admire the brunette's backside as she walks away, irrationally willing her to turn around and glance at me, but she keeps walking, face forward, toward the back of the bar.

Well, shit. Am I deluding myself? I would have sworn that was Hot Teacher.

With my heart sinking into my toes, I turn around and try to flag down the busy bartender—a dapper guy with tattoos on both forearms and the bluest eyes I've ever seen. Jesus. No wonder the hot brunette didn't bother to look at me when she was talking to this guy. If I were her, he'd have had my full attention, too.

"Hey, man," the bartender says, coming to a stop in front of me with a smile. "What can I get you, brother?"

I look at his nametag. "Hey, Ryan. Do you remember the elegant brunette sitting on the end a few minutes ago?"

"Red dress?"

I nod. "Could you make another of whatever she was drinking?"

"Extra-dirty vodka martini. You've got it. Anything else?"

I place the rest of my order: drinks for Max and me, plus enough shots for both the birthday girl's and the hot brunette's groups. As the bartender gets to work, I turn and scan the room. The place is too packed for me to spot Max or the brunette and her friends, so I use the opportunity to carefully survey the crowd, in case it was only wishful thinking that the hot brunette is my mystery woman.

Hmm. Age-wise, there are other possibilities—women who'd fit the bill. And some of them are attractive to me. But nobody else even comes close to jolting me the way the hot brunette did. If you ask me, she's in a league of her own.

"Order up," the bartender says behind me.

I turn around and pay the man, and he helps me place the multitude of glasses onto a large tray. First off, I deliver a round of tequila shots to the rowdy young women and blush when they crowd around me and pinch my cheeks in thanks.

"Have fun, ladies," I say, turning to go with my tray. To my surprise, they beg me to stay and join their party. But I shake my head. "Thanks, but I'm here to meet someone," I explain. "I'm off to deliver the rest of these drinks to her and her friends."

They wish me well and drift away, while I carefully make my way through the crowded room in search of Max and the women.

Well, fuck.

It's a good news/bad news situation. The good news is that Max has secured a two-top for us that happens to be located immediately next to a much larger table occupied by none other than the hot brunette and her elegant friends. The bad news, however, is that Max is currently directing the full force of his legendary smolder toward one woman in particular at that next table—the same hot brunette I'm fervently hoping is the sexy, kind, and confident MILF I've come here tonight to sweep off her feet.

3
SELENA

I watch Grayson walking in my direction with a tray full of drinks, which surprises me. Did he come here with a big group of friends, or is he planning to drink all of that himself? I must say, he's even cuter in person than in his photos. Taller than I would have expected, and, in person, kindness radiates off that boy like a physical thing.

Now that I've seen him, I'm not surprised he doesn't fare well on dating apps. A girl needs to see this cutie in person to fully appreciate his sweet brand of sex appeal. He's got no game, clearly, like he said during our text exchange. The beaming, sweet smile he flashed me earlier confirmed "what you see is what you get" with this adorable boy. But I think transparency could be his greatest strength, if only he'd embrace it without apology.

"Older women know who they are and what they want, you know?" the guy at the adjacent table says. He's been trying to chat me up since we sat down. "I like that they don't play games."

"If you say so," I say. But my eyes are focused firmly on Grayson as he nears my table with that tray of drinks. Has he mustered the courage to come straight for me? Are all those drinks for my friends and me? From the moment our eyes locked earlier, it seemed pretty clear he figured I was Hot Teacher, but I never would have thought he'd be certain enough about that hunch to beeline over here with a tray of drinks. Bravo, my little Grayson-hopper!

"Hey, Grayson, what took you so long?" the cocky guy at the next table says, making me realize my little Grayson-hopper isn't heading straight for my table, after all.

Grayson's eyes meet mine as he reaches his friend and puts down his tray. This time, however, Grayson doesn't smile at me like a toddler beholding a rainbow pony. Unlike last time, Grayson apparently has decided to wait for me to confirm my identity before making another move.

"What's up with all the shots?" the slick guy at the next table asks.

Grayson looks at his friend, making me regret I didn't out myself with a "you got me!" smile before he looked away. "They're for all these beautiful ladies," Grayson explains before addressing my table as a whole. "It's packed tonight and hard to get the bartender's attention, so I figured I'd get a bunch of shots for you ladies if you'd like them."

"How sweet of you," my friend, Marnie, says.

"My pleasure," Grayson replies, his heart-melting face a deep shade of crimson. As my friends grab shots off the tray, Grayson holds out a glass to me. "I got this vodka martini for you, if you'd like it. I noticed you sitting at the bar earlier, so I asked the bartender to make you another round."

Okay, that's it. With that charming move, this cutie pie has made it impossible for me to play it cool a second longer. "Thank you so much . . . *Grayson*."

His face lights up. "I knew it!"

I chuckle. "What a smooth move, my little Grayson-hopper.

Bravo." I wink and take a sip of the martini. "Mm. It's extra-dirty. Exactly the way I like it."

Grayson opens and closes his mouth, too overcome to speak, and I can't help fawning over his adorableness with my best friend, Victoria, sitting next to me.

"Is this the little friend you told us about, Selena?" Victoria asks.

"This is him. Isn't he darling?" I look Grayson up and down. "But he's not so little, is he?" Laughing, I stand and open my arms. "It's great to see you, Grayson. Thanks for convincing me to meet you."

Grayson embraces me. "Thanks for being convincible."

"It was a losing battle. You were *very* persuasive."

I pull a chair to Grayson's small table and sit next to him, across from his handsome buddy who's currently looking deeply perplexed.

"How on earth did you figure me out?" I ask coyly. "There are plenty of women around my age at the bar tonight."

Grayson is absolutely beaming. "I recognized you the second I saw you," he declares proudly. "Not physically, obviously. It was your energy. Your confidence. You were everything I imagined Hot Teacher would be, and then some."

"*Hot Teacher?*" his cocky friend mutters, but we both ignore him.

"Stop," I say flirtatiously to Grayson while playfully batting his forearm. "And by that, I mean, 'Please, tell me more.'"

Grayson chuckles. "You're gorgeous, *Selena*. That's your name?" He must have overheard Victoria calling me that earlier. When I nod, Grayson asks, "Why didn't you acknowledge me when you saw me smiling like a dork at you earlier?"

"Oh, you smiled at me?" I say mischievously.

Grayson scoffs playfully. "Don't pretend you didn't notice the goofy smile that involuntarily took control of my mouth the second you looked at me."

I bite my lower lip. "Yes, I noticed it. How could I miss a wide, beaming, no-holds-barred smile like that?" I lean in and touch his forearm again. "To be honest, I wanted to check out your flirting game from afar for a little while. I'm here to give you tips, after all."

"God, I hope that's not why you're here," Grayson says, leaning closer to me and smiling with noticeable heat. "That is, unless you're planning to give me tips on flirting with *you*."

My heart skips a beat. "It doesn't seem like you need any help with that, my dear. To my surprise, you're doing fabulously well on your own."

His green eyes sparkle. "Says the woman who looked away when I smiled directly at her."

I shrug. "For all I knew, you smile like a kid on Christmas at every woman who makes eye contact with you in a bar. I needed more information before revealing myself."

To my relief, Grayson hoots with laughter at my comment, rather than looking offended. "Actually, I usually react like *this* when a woman looks at me in a bar." He makes a face like he just stuck his finger into a light socket. "I only smile like a kid on Christmas when the woman is as gorgeous as you—which has only happened once in my entire life, because you're in a class by yourself, Selena."

I hoot and clap. "And you claim to be bad at flirting?"

"I am," Grayson says.

"He is," his buddy confirms. But, again, we both ignore him.

"Speaking of flirting," I say. "You seemed to be flirting like a boss with those pretty, young women by the bar. I noticed at least a couple of them looking you up and down with interest. One of them even pinched your cheeks. Were you able to get any phone numbers out of them, Grayson-hopper—hopefully, real ones this time?"

Grayson rolls his eyes. "If any of those women appeared to

be flirting with me, it was only because they'd chosen me as their next mark."

I furrow my brow. "Their *mark*?"

He nods. "They figured I'd be a shoo-in to buy them a round of drinks."

"And were they right about that?"

"What do you think?"

I burst out laughing. "Oh, Grayson."

"I didn't do it because I was interested in any of them, if that's what you're thinking. I did it so I could get past them as quickly as possible and talk to *you*—the hot brunette at the bar."

I flash him a look that says, "Sure."

"It's true! Okay, yes, I probably *also* did it out of sheer force of habit and politeness. It's not like me to say no in a situation like that. But, mostly, I was trying to get my ass to the bar to talk to the smoking-hot brunette in the red dress who'd commanded my full attention the minute I laid eyes on her."

"Will you introduce me, Gray?" the slick guy interjects. He motions to Grayson and me. "I take it you two already know each other?"

"Yes, Grayson and I met online earlier today," I explain, deciding that's all the man needs to know. "He invited me for a drink, and I found him way too charming and handsome to refuse, even though I don't usually date men his age." I flash a seductive smile at Grayson, not only to give Grayson a little tingle in his trousers but to let Mr. Slick know he should find someone else to hit on.

"Selena, this is Max," Grayson says. His cheeks are flushed. Clearly, my seductive smile a moment ago hit its target.

"Would you boys like to join our table?" I ask. "There's plenty of room."

"I thought you'd never ask," Grayson replies. He looks at Mr. Slick, who nods enthusiastically, and a moment later,

Grayson is placing the remaining drinks on my table while his buddy drags over two chairs.

In short order, both men get settled at my table— with Grayson sitting next to me and his friend next to my gregarious friend, Marnie, at her invitation. Easy conversation among the full table ensues for a while, and through it all I can't stop marveling at how funny and darling Grayson is with my friends. Indeed, throughout the energetic group conversation, my best friend since college, Victoria, keeps shooting me secret winks and smiles, letting me know she finds Grayson every bit as yummy and likeable as I'd described to our group earlier at dinner.

After a bit, individual conversations begin breaking off from the group, with Marnie and Max chatting together and Grayson and me leaning in and talking intimately for about a half-hour.

"Tell me something," I say to Grayson after we've been conversing one-on-one for a while. "What if the brunette in the red dress—the woman you were bold enough to buy a drink before ever saying a word to her—hadn't turned out to be Hot Teacher?"

"I knew you were Hot Teacher."

"But what if it turned out you'd been wrong about that? What if the *real* Hot Teacher had walked through the front door while you were buying all those drinks? What if she beelined up to you and said, 'It's me, Grayson!'? Would you have ditched Hot Teacher to bring me that martini or the other way around?"

Grayson scoffs. "This is a pointless hypothetical because I knew, instantly, you were Hot Teacher. I knew it in my bones. On my skin. In my gut." He leans forward. "*And in my pants*."

Whoa. When did this slightly dorky dude get so fucking hot?

Before I've decided how to respond to Grayson's bold comment, my friend Marnie stands at the other end of our table. "Max and I are going outside to smoke."

As Max rises from the table, he shoots a sly little wink at

Grayson that practically screams, "Someone's gonna get lucky tonight!" before turning and gesturing to Marnie. "After you."

And off they go. First, to smoke. And second, to fuck, if I know Marnie.

"Well, damn," Victoria says, snorting. "I didn't see that one coming."

"Max is really smooth," Grayson explains earnestly, obviously not realizing Victoria's comment was sarcastic. Unbeknownst to sweet Grayson, she wasn't complimenting Max's prowess with women but, rather, making a joke borne of love and admiration about our darling Marnie's propensity for unabashedly going after whatever and whomever she desires.

"I was being sarcastic, sweetie," Victoria explains to Grayson with a smile. "This ain't Marnie's first rodeo with a young cowboy. She just went through a bad breakup, so she's been getting over that guy by getting under—and over, and in front of, and sitting on the faces of—some young, highly energetic cowboys."

Grayson looks absolutely stunned. "Oh, yeah, no. Good for her. I'm all for sex positivity." He awkwardly fist-pumps the air, making all the women at our table giggle. He continues, "I just meant Max always seems to be catnip to women, wherever we go, so I'm not at all surprised Marnie decided to leave with him."

I place my hand on Grayson's thigh underneath the table. "Your friend isn't catnip to me. In fact, he's not my type at all."

Grayson's chest heaves. "No?" When I shake my head, he swallows hard and breathlessly asks, "What *is* your type? Because whatever it is, Selena, I'm at your service to be that tonight."

Victoria guffaws. "Well played, Grayson." She winks at me. "He might not be subtle, Selena. And he's certainly not smooth, by any stretch. But he's enthusiastic and fucking adorable."

"He sure is." I side-eye Grayson for a long beat, warning him not to get ahead of himself, but it's clear from his facial expression he's going to explode if I don't answer his implied invitation soon. I remind him, "I told you I'm not looking for anything serious."

"You did. Understood."

"I didn't say that to play hard to get. I genuinely don't have room in my life, or in my heart, for a boyfriend or any kind of serious commitment. Frankly, I'm worried you're the kind of guy who falls hard and fast."

"Thank you. That's an accurate assessment."

I laugh, making him chuckle.

"But you're being clear with me going in, and I know exactly what I'm getting myself into. I've heard your terms and conditions, Hot Teacher, and promise to abide by all of them." He holds up three fingers. "Scout's honor."

"That's only meaningful if you were actually a Boy Scout."

"I was."

I chuckle. "Of course, you were."

Grayson's green eyes are twinkling. His dimples popping. "Come on, Selena. Our chemistry is through the roof. Let's do this."

I bite my lip. I want to say yes so badly, but I'm thoroughly enjoying torturing him. "Let's do *what*?" I ask seductively. "That's the question."

With his green eyes flickering, Grayson leans into my ear and shocks me by whispering, "Whatever the fuck you want, all night long."

Arousal floods me. It zaps my most sensitive nerve endings and makes my nipples harden. I say, "You promise you won't get your mind blown by me, fall hard, and then bomb me with texts and calls? Don't you dare make me block your number or file a restraining order, Grayson."

He briefly ponders my comment. "Okay, I can't in good conscience promise *not* to get my mind blown by you. I'm positive I will. I also can't promise *not* to fall hard for you. It's highly likely. But I *do* promise I won't bomb you with texts and calls afterwards. I do promise you won't need to block me or file a restraining order. I do promise to respect your boundaries, no matter what." As before, he holds up three fingers and adds, "Scout's honor. And who knows? Maybe, once you're done blowing my mind, I'll be chomping at the bit to bite the next lucky lady's ass."

I burst into laughter and squeeze his thigh under the table. "Okay, you've convinced me. Let's do this."

With a whoop, he fist-pumps the air and jolts to standing.

"Bye, kids," Victoria says as Grayson pulls me up. Before we've walked away, she motions for me to lean in to hear a private comment, and when my ear is at my best friend's lips, she whispers, "I'll never forgive you, if you don't give me a full report in the morning."

4
SELENA

"Would you like a room with a view, Ms. Diaz?" the hotel clerk behind the counter asks.

"Actually, why don't you upgrade me to a suite with a view, if you've got one available," I reply. Why not? Even though Grayson and I are only going to be staying at this hotel for one glorious night of fun, we might as well shag in style.

With Drew at Andre's the whole weekend, I theoretically could have brought Grayson back to my empty house to fuck his brains out there. But I'd never bring a man home, not even one as seemingly gentle and non-threatening as Grayson. The last thing I need is for Grayson to fall for me after I've blown his twenty-five-year-old dick and mind tonight and then, to my mortification, start showing up at my front door like a lost puppy, fruitlessly determined to woo me. Good lord, the very thought sends my pulse through the roof, and not in a good way.

"Let me pay for the upgrade, at least," Grayson says, holding up his credit card once again. But same as last time, I gently push his hand away.

"I've got plenty of points to cover everything." I turn my head and wink covertly at the hotel clerk, nonverbally instructing her not to contradict my little white lie to Grayson, and my cute little boy toy begrudgingly thanks me and slides his credit card back into his beat-up wallet.

I know Grayson fervently wants to be a gentleman and pay for our room tonight, the same way he paid for all those drinks at the bar, but there's no way I'd let him do that. This luxury hotel —picked by *me,* not him—is outrageously expensive, and I'm sure the bill for even one night would hit Grayson pretty hard in that beat-up wallet of his.

For one thing, it's apparent Grayson McKnight wasn't born with a silver spoon in his mouth, but, rather, has had to work hard for every penny in his bank account. At the bar, Grayson mentioned his mother is a high school English teacher and that he's never had a relationship with his father. At one point, he also mentioned he lives in a small apartment that doesn't allow pets, and that he's saving up "little by little" to buy a condo where a big dog would have at least some patio space in which to hang out.

In terms of *how* Grayson has worked for those hard-earned pennies, Grayson and I haven't talked in detail about our careers. At the bar, I merely said I'm a "design consultant" and Grayson said he "works in IT." But based on a few of his stories, I got the distinct impression Grayson is working at the same job he landed out of college three years ago, which means it's probably still an entry-level position, or close to it—and that deduction was only reinforced when Grayson said he interviewed last week for a "huge" promotion at work.

"Here you go, Ms. Diaz," the clerk says, sliding my credit card and a key card to me.

"Thank you." I smile at Grayson. "Come with me, Mr. McKnight." I take his hand, and off we go toward the elevators at the far end of the lobby, both of us grinning with excited anticipation.

When we reach our room, I swipe the keycard against the

lock, and Grayson and I tumble inside, both of us practically pawing at each other like hungry wolves. When the door closes behind us, Grayson backs me into it, crushing his lips to mine.

As his tongue slides into my mouth and begins leading mine in a swirling dance, I feverishly curl my thigh around his hips and press my center against his hard bulge, spurring him on. And that's all it takes for both of us to become a frenzied, devouring blur of lustful lips, tongues, and hands.

"You're such a good kisser!" I blurt excitedly, yanking up furiously on Grayson's Henley shirt.

"Because I'm kissing *you*," he says.

With a gleam in his green eyes that can only be described as feral, Grayson rips off his long-sleeved shirt, revealing a youthful, lean torso and lightly sculpted arms—one of which is covered in a tattoo sleeve. Grayson's body isn't what I'd call ripped. He's obviously not a "gym bro" or a likely candidate to grace the cover of a men's fitness magazine. But standing before me now, his chest heaving and his eyes blazing with heat, everything about Grayson's body and energy is screaming "Virile! Healthy! Fit! *Hot*!"—all of which is making me physically salivate at the sight of him.

"You're so *sexy*, Grayson-hopper," I breathe, running my palm over a slight patch of hair between his pecs. "Show me the rest."

Without hesitation, Grayson quickly strips off his shoes, pants, and socks, practically tripping over himself as he does, and then furiously pulls my dress up and off like it's on fire. And just like that, we're standing mere inches apart in nothing but our underwear.

"Jesus, Hot Teacher," he says, looking me up and down. He licks his lips before fixing his eyes on mine. "You're a goddess. Fucking *perfect*."

I can barely breathe. Not every man wants a woman built like me. I don't often see my body type represented as "sexy" in

Hollywood and popular media. But there's no doubt Grayson is genuinely salivating at the sight of me. Indeed, the look of pure, unadulterated appreciation on his face as he drinks in my every curve sends butterflies whooshing into my belly. So much so, I suddenly feel like I'm physically swooning.

I grab onto his arm to keep myself steady, as he leans down and devours my lace-covered breasts. As he kisses me, he reaches around and unlatches my bra, and when my breasts are freed from their bondage, he yelps with appreciation, before diving straight into my abundant cleavage and erect nipples.

After ravenously licking and sucking my nipples and breasts, Grayson takes my hand and pulls me to the bed, murmuring as we go that I'm "hot" and "perfect" and that he's in heaven. His breathing ragged and his skin practically glowing with his attraction to me, he lays me down on my back, crawls alongside me on the bed, and devours every inch of my torso, belly, hips, breasts, and neck, all while stroking between my legs, on the outside of my lace underwear.

As my arousal becomes more and more apparent, Grayson slides a hand inside my panties and dips a couple fingers inside my wetness, at which point, I'm so fucking aroused, I can't help crying out at his delicious invasion of my body, like I've just gripped an electric fence.

"I want you so badly," I gasp out, my hips gyrating with the movement of his fingers inside me.

"Oh God, Selena. You're so fucking hot."

"*You're* so fucking hot," I whisper. "How'd you get so good at this?" I add, referring to the exquisite motion of his fingers. Surely, I've never been touched this brilliantly in all my life.

As he kisses and touches me, I begin stroking the straining bulge behind his briefs, surprised by his impressive size. The man is well over six feet tall, so I've been assuming he'd be relatively "to scale" down there. But what I'm feeling behind the fabric of Grayson's briefs is longer and thicker than I would have expected, with a particularly beefy tip that's surely going to feel amazing when it stretches my opening and leads the way for the rest of him.

I tug on his underwear, ravenous to feel that impressive bulge stretching and filling me. "Fuck me," I purr. "Take 'em off."

With a loud groan, Grayson yanks off his underwear, allowing his straining cock to spring free and defy gravity, and the sight of his huge, veiny erection teetering before me is enough to make me whimper with excitement. As suspected from the feel of him, my sweet little Grayson-hopper ain't so little between his legs. In fact, he's a *very* big boy. Bonus points? His beefy, shiny tip is already beaded with sexy pre-cum, which tells me he's every bit as ramped up as I am.

My skin alive with excitement, I rip off my underwear, rather than waiting for him to do it, which causes him to mutter something appreciative under his breath and push me back flat onto the bed. As I writhe on the mattress, my body clearly inviting him to fuck me, he spreads my thighs wide, crawls between my legs, and starts eating me with unbridled enthusiasm, before quickly adding his fingers to the mix—until soon, I feel like I'm about to be shot out of a fucking cannon.

"Oh, God," I blurt, gripping Grayson's head as he eats voraciously between my legs. "Don't stop," I gasp out. "Keep going, just like this. Oh, fuck, Grayson. This is so gooooood."

Andre hated performing oral sex on me. The rare times he deigned to do it, it was so damned easy to tell he wasn't into it, I almost always wound up faking an orgasm to get it over with, since telling him to stop once he'd started would have pissed him off. Since then, the various men I've slept with have been hit or miss in this department. But even the "hits" never hit the ball out of the park, the way this hungry, enthusiastic, surprisingly *talented* boy is doing. Holy hell, Grayson isn't merely hitting a homerun between my legs. He's hitting a grand slam in the bottom of the ninth!

As my pleasure rises and spirals, my core begins increasingly tightening, until it feels like I'm going to snap and shoot into the stratosphere. As my pleasure rises and rises, I grip anything and everything I can, furiously, to keep myself from getting smashed by the impending tidal wave hovering over me. I fist Grayson's hair. Then grip his ears. I clutch the white comforter underneath me on the hotel bed, paradoxically fending off the pleasure that's threatening to break me in half, while also desperately wanting to relax enough to surrender and get utterly thrashed by it.

"You taste so fucking good," Grayson coos between licks and swirls of his tongue and lips, his fingers mercilessly continuing their rhythmic assault.

When I moan my desperate reply, he chuckles and dives into his meal again, never for a moment stopping that magical thing he's doing with his fingers inside me.

All of a sudden, my core muscles tighten and flex, like they're poised and ready to release. And that's when Grayson slides a fingertip inside my anus, instantly hurtling my body into a release so extreme, so exquisite, so all-consuming and body-quaking, I can't help bursting into tears as my body is wracked with wave after wave of ecstasy.

When the pleasure finally stops throttling me, and my spirit has finally stopped soaring around the hotel room and rejoined my body, I arch my back and spread my legs even wider, desperate for Grayson to fuck me with that gorgeous cock of his. But to my surprise, he *still* doesn't take the bait, but instead lies alongside me on the bed, and once again slides his fingers inside me. My clit is throbbing and sensitive at the moment, so I'm poised and ready to coach him not to touch me there. But to my surprise, he doesn't need the guidance. In fact, he clearly doesn't need any instruction at all, as he leaves my clit alone and begins dragging his fingers firmly across my G-spot, over and over again, while whispering a string of dirty talk into my ear.

I'm intrigued by his attempt to coax another orgasm from me prior to intercourse, but I'm not hopeful he'll succeed. As good as this thing he's doing with his fingers feels, I'm certain the only thing that could get me off again is that cock of his, thrusting deep inside me and banging on the very spot he's currently—

Oh, Jesus.

Whoa.

Wow.

What the hell is happening to me?

Out of nowhere, I feel a sharp tightening inside me again. Only this time, even more acutely, and from an even deeper place inside me than before.

I grip the comforter beneath me, steadying myself for the orgasm that's clearly going to throttle me, any minute now, while Grayson's breathing next to me becomes ragged with increased excitement.

"You're a goddess," he whispers into my ear, as his fingers manipulate me without mercy. "You're perfect, Selena. I can't wait to fuck you."

With that, he speeds up the tempo of his fingers inside me, ever so slightly, causing my toes to curl and my eyes to roll back. A second later, a tsunami of pleasure crashes inside me, sending waves of ecstasy ripping through me.

As I scream and writhe, Grayson bites my hard nipples. And when my orgasm subsides, he breathlessly grabs one of the condoms we stopped to purchase on the way here, crawls over me on the bed, brings my thighs to rest on his shoulders, places his thick mushroom tip at my wet, yearning entrance, and, with his eyes laser-focused on mine, burrows his thick cock deep, deep, deep inside me, all the way, making me growl with pleasure as he stretches and fills me to the absolute brink.

As Grayson's body rocks in and out of mine, I clutch his forearms feverishly, reveling in every delicious sensation. As his thrusts pick up steam and become animalistic, as our moans become louder and more desperate, I reach through a gap in our gyrating bodies and caress his balls and taint, instantly driving him to obvious madness.

But just when I think he's going to come undone, Grayson abruptly pulls out of me, panting like an Olympic sprinter. With a sexy grunt, he flips me over onto my hands and knees, and begins eating me out from behind, while simultaneously fucking me with his fingers.

Holy fucking shit!

I never would have guessed the mild-mannered man from the bar would fuck like a goddamned beast! I thought I'd have to take the lead and coach him through some basics, which I wouldn't have minded doing at all. But nope. Here I am, having the best sex of my life—on the cusp of coming an unheard of *third* time—and I haven't had to teach this talented boy a goddamned thing!

As I continue moaning and trying not to crash face-first into the mattress, Grayson suddenly does something that shocks me. Something that *shouldn't* shock me, given our text conversation, but apparently I'm not in my right mind at the moment. *He bites my ass.* And, holy hell, it has the exact effect on me I told him it would.

"You're so fucking delicious," he mutters behind me, his voice husky. "I want to devour every fucking inch of you, Selena."

As I yelp my enthusiastic reply, he thankfully plunges his full length inside me—so deeply from our new position, I can't help crying out in reply in ecstasy and shock.

Grayson thrusts once, twice, three times. *Hard.* With his hands gripping my hips to ensure maximum depth of his body's invasion. And, just like that, I'm wracked by an explosion of pleasure that's so intense, it sends warm liquid physically spurting out of me from the precise spot Grayson is fucking me. Did I just *squirt*?

Not surprisingly, Grayson comes right after me, reaching around to pinch my nipple, as he does. Until, finally, we both collapse onto the bed into a sweaty, tangled, breathless heap.

"Jesus," I mutter. "Damn."

"Leave Jesus out of it," he retorts. "That was all me, baby."

I giggle. "Sorry. You're so right. *Grayson.* Damn."

He slides off me, pointedly looking toward the nightstand. So, I look over there, too, assuming he's looking at the clock. Currently, it reads 12:37.

"When's check-out tomorrow?" he asks.

"Eleven, I think."

He sighs with disappointment. And I can't deny, I'm feeling the same way. After sex that good, if I could stop time and spend the entire week in this hotel room with this hunky man, I'd leap at the chance.

"Do you think we could get a late check-out?" he asks. "I mean, if you don't have somewhere you need to be in the morning. Since this is only a one-time thing, I want to maximize my classroom time with you, Hot Teacher."

I giggle and place my palm on his bare chest. "There's no need for you to call me that anymore, honey. At least, when it comes to sex. Obviously, you don't need the slightest bit of instruction from me."

His smile would light up the night sky. "Really?"

"I swear on a stack of bibles. You think I come like that—and three times—during mediocre sex? Uh, no."

Grayson rubs his palms together and laughs like cartoon villain, yet again making me giggle.

"I'll call down and ask for a late check-out now," I say. I reach for the phone on the nightstand and place the call, and when I hang up, Grayson hoots and fist-pumps the air, like he's just won the lottery.

"You're definitely not playing it cool, are you?" I say, laughing.

"How could I possibly play it cool at a time like this," he says, "after being granted more valuable time with the world's most beautiful woman? A pulchritudinous goddess beyond compare."

"I'm a *what* goddess?"

Grayson rolls onto his side and takes my hand in his. "*Pulchritudinous*. It's just a fancy way of saying 'beautiful.' I figure you've been called 'beautiful' and 'gorgeous' and 'stunning' too many times to count in your lifetime, so I'm trying to find a word that's never been said to you before."

I swoon. "Well, mission accomplished. I'm quite certain you're the first man to call me that. I've never even heard the word before."

I'd never admit this to Grayson, but the truth is I haven't been called "beautiful" or "gorgeous" or "stunning" countless times. Not by a long shot. In fact, I'm deeply ashamed of how long I put up with being called "stupid" and "ugly" and "fat" in my marriage with Andre. But why on earth would I reveal that to Grayson and cast a pall over this magical, sexy night?

Grayson looks extremely pleased with my response. "Awesome," he says, his green eyes sparkling in the low light of our hotel room. "Now, if ever you hear that fancy word again, you'll hopefully think of me and the wrong number that brought us together for one perfectly *pulchritudinous* night."

5
SELENA

I sigh with deep-seated sexual satisfaction and grin at adorable, sweaty Grayson lying next to me. Who knew the sweet guy whose rambling dinner invitation to "Katie" would turn out to be such a freaking wildebeest in the sack? By a country mile, he's easily the best sex partner I've ever had!

If I thought that first, explosive romp with Grayson would turn out to be a novelty—a perfect storm of combustion, never to be repeated again—I was dead wrong. As it's turned out, our second and third times have been every bit as electrifying. Even better, in fact, as we've quickly learned each other's bodies and cues.

Plus, in between all the amazing sex, I never would have dreamed I'd enjoy chatting and laughing with Grayson as much as I have. In fact, when we're not fucking, Grayson and I can't stop chattering away, quickly discovering we have a lot in common. For instance, we both love sports, reading, and hiking. We both adore trying new restaurants and watching the same kinds of shows. And we both love animals, especially dogs.

"I'm not going to be able to move tomorrow," I say, rearranging my naked body among our tangled sheets to press myself against him.

"Oh, no, does that mean you're tapping out?" he asks. "Because I'm sure I could go at least one more time before check-out, given a little time to recharge my battery."

I glance at the clock on the nightstand, which reads 4:44, and my heart physically squeezes at the thought that I'll need to say goodbye to this gorgeous man in mere hours.

"Of course, I'm not tapping out," I say. "I'm game to go as many times as you can. Give me all you've got."

"*Nice*." He chuckles. "So, do you have any feedback for me? I know you said I don't need to call you Hot Teacher anymore, but, seriously, if there's anything I can do to improve next time, I want to hear it."

I run my fingertips over Grayson's bare chest, tracing his nipple in the moonlight. "Nope. You're doing things to my body *nobody* has ever done before. If anything, you should be telling *me* what I can do better."

"Not a goddamned thing. You're sheer perfection." He pauses. "Have I really done things to you, nobody else has ever done?"

"You think I always react like this? Ha! Some guys I've been with literally don't even know to touch my clit."

He scoffs. "*What*? Dude, what's wrong with them?"

"I really don't know. Are they really selfish or really stupid? It's anyone's guess."

"Jesus. The best techniques for making a woman come are all right there on the internet! There's this guy on YouTube called Ball Peen Hammer who literally gives step-by-step instructions!"

"*Really*?"

"Oh, yeah. He has tons of videos, explaining what to do. As it turns out, based on how many orgasms you've had, his techniques are spot-on." He snickers. "Or I guess they're *G*-spot on, huh?"

The implication of what he's just said dawns on me. "Wait, so you're saying . . . before me, you'd never tried out these techniques before? I'm the first woman to reap the benefits of the video tutorials you've watched?"

Grayson blushes, apparently realizing what he's admitted to me.

I sit up and look down at his face in the moonlight. "Grayson, am I your first? Were you a virgin when we walked into this room?"

He looks flustered. "No, of course not! I was with my ex-girlfriend for five years, remember? We were each other's firsts. She wasn't all that adventurous, though. She'd been through some bad stuff as a kid and had a lot of hang-ups about sex and her body. Obviously, I tried to be supportive and as gentle as possible with her, always, but no matter what approach I took, we really never had a great sex life. After we broke up, I made it my mission to study up, so I'd be able to hit the ball out of the park with a new partner, if, God willing, I ever got the opportunity."

"And hit the ball out of the park, you did, my dear. If only Katie knew what she missed out on, she'd be kicking herself right now."

"Stupid Katie."

I swirl my fingertip through the little patch of hair between his pecs. "So . . . am I understanding this right: I'm only the *second* woman you've ever slept with?"

Grayson blushes, telegraphing the answer to my question is *yes*. "That's a turn-off, right? I shouldn't admit that."

"Is it the truth?"

He nods. "Not for a lack of trying, though. I keep getting fake numbers."

My stomach clenches. I could tell this boy was the type to

fall hard and fast, but this new revelation makes me realize this hookup will likely be even more significant for Grayson than I'd imagined.

"Shit. I've blown it, haven't I?" he says, reacting to whatever he's seeing on my face. "I should have lied. Fuck. What number should I say in the future, if a woman asks me how many women I've been with? Five? Ten? It should be a big enough number that I don't sound like a total loser, the way I just did with you, but not *so* big that I sound like a Max-level douchebag."

"You're not a loser, Grayson," I say, touching his cheek. "Never lie, okay? You are who you are and don't have anything to be embarrassed about. If anything, your sexual history only makes me even more impressed with your amazing skills. I was a virgin when I married my husband, while he was very experienced—and he was never even close to as talented a lover as you. Not back when I lost my virginity to him, and not after twelve years of marriage, during which he was having multiple affairs."

"Seriously?"

I nod. "Obviously, a man having lots of sexual partners doesn't necessarily mean he's skilled. I think it's more about the man's philosophy. Does he like giving pleasure, or does he only care about receiving it? With my ex, sex was only ever about *his* pleasure, and nothing else. He'd only ever give me oral sex on very special occasions. And when he did, not surprisingly, he totally sucked at it."

"What the fuck?"

I shrug. "Since I'd never been with anyone but him, I thought that was totally normal behavior for a very long time. I thought there was something wrong with me, because sex wasn't all that thrilling to me. But then, I started reading romance novels and erotica, and talking to my friends, and I realized my ex was just a horrible, selfish lover, and I was an extremely sexual person who needed some actual foreplay before he shoved it in!"

Grayson grimaces. "That sounds horrible. I'm so glad you got out of that marriage."

"Sounds like it was a good thing you got out of your relationship, too."

"Yeah, it was." He pauses. "Being with you has shown me, so clearly, what I'm looking for in my next relationship." His eyes widen. "Which I know won't be with you. Don't worry. All I'm saying is being with you has shown me how fun it is to be with a woman who's comfortable in her own sexuality. That's what I want for myself. It's so fun, making you feel so damned good. I feel like a superhero."

"I hope you find a girlfriend like that, Grayson. You deserve to feel like a superhero—in and out of bed."

He smiles ruefully. "Thanks."

Aw, Grayson. Obviously, he's poking around a bit, trying to figure out if I've magically changed my mind about not wanting a boyfriend.

I touch his arm. "Honey, this wouldn't work out. We're at totally different stages of our lives. You're looking for that special person to settle down with. Maybe you even want to have a kid one day. But I've already done all that. I like being free and not having to consider anyone's schedule or feelings but mine and my son's and my dog's."

Grayson considers that for a long beat, and finally nods and says, "Can I see a photo of this dog you're always talking about? She sounds amazing."

"With pleasure."

I pull out my phone and show Grayson a photo, which thankfully launches our conversation into an entirely different direction. He asks to see more photos, so I show him all my favorite snapshots and videos, beginning from when I got Daisy as a puppy three years ago, and Grayson makes comments and asks questions that turn me into a giggling, gushing chatterbox.

Soon, our conversation about Daisy leads to a broader one about our childhood dogs, which then leads us to talking about our families and childhoods. And through it all, I can't help marveling at how easy it is to talk to Grayson. With him, I feel cracked wide open in a way I've never felt with any man. I feel safe and seen. Sexy and desirable. I feel totally and completely natural and comfortable.

"Do you look more like your mother or father?" he asks, in the midst of a conversation about how close I've always been with my father, since my mother died when I was eight.

"I look exactly like my mother," I say.

"I look like my mother, too," he says. "Does Drew look like you?"

"He does. He's my mini-me!"

"Lucky kid. Can I see a photo?"

I freeze. It's a natural question, given the way our conversation has flowed. So, I don't blame him for asking it. But I can't believe I've allowed Drew to become a casual topic of our conversation! I never bring up my son to a date, other than to perhaps acknowledge his existence.

"I don't think that'd be a good idea," I say. "Sorry. I don't normally share much about my life with Drew with a date. I like keeping my life as a mother separate from whatever fun I have while Drew is at his father's house."

Grayson's face falls sharply, making me realize what I've just implied—namely, that tonight with him is still nothing to me but a little "fun." Yes, it started out that way. But I can't honestly say, after spending all this time with him, not only having sex, but having deep and meaningful conversations, too, that I haven't felt a profound shift between us. An emotional connection that's been growing and becoming more and more apparent, with each passing hour.

Indeed, in the short amount of time I've spent with Grayson, both via text and in person, he's already managed to touch my heart, every bit as much as he's given my body new kinds of pleasure. But I really shouldn't admit any of that to him, because I can't fathom a path forward with him, beyond tonight, that makes a lick of rational sense.

"I understand," he says, referring to my comment about Drew. But the look of disappointment on his face makes me want to explain further, so he knows my reluctance to open up completely with him has nothing to do with him.

"My divorce was brutal, not only on me, but on Drew, too," I say. "My ex went after full custody, not because he actually wanted to be a full-time parent, but because he wanted to pay me as little child support as possible. The whole thing was terribly hard on Drew, because he only wanted to live with me. He said so, over and over again."

"Ugh. That's tough."

"Thankfully, the judge listened to Drew and gave me primary physical custody, with joint legal custody, and we've now managed to work out a schedule that everyone is good with. But ever since the divorce, I've made it my top priority for Drew to know he's got at least one parent who always puts him first, no matter what. As part of that, I don't introduce him to anyone I'm seeing. I don't ever want him getting attached to someone who won't be around forever."

"I totally get it. I think you're a great mom."

"Thank you. My ex introduces Drew to a different girlfriend every other month—some of them younger than you. Last week, he brought his latest to Drew's basketball game, and Drew said he couldn't fully concentrate with her in the stands."

"Your ex sounds like a real winner." He twists his mouth. "Just throwing this out there. If you ever want to give your ex a taste of his own medicine and parade your new boy toy around in front of him, then I absolutely volunteer as tribute. Not in front of Drew, of course. We'd have to engineer a way to 'bump into him,' while out on a date."

Oh, Grayson. The man will do anything to ensure he sees me again after tonight. And I can't deny I want that, too. In fact, the thought of saying goodbye to him, in mere hours, makes my heart physically squeeze.

"Thanks for the offer. I appreciate it. I'll definitely think about it."

I can't fathom I'd ever parade Grayson around in front of my ex-husband. Fuck Andre. But I do appreciate Grayson's willingness to do anything he can to make me feel good. With a wicked smile, I begin walking my fingers playfully up his belly to the hairy indentation between his pecs. "So, hey, here's a thought . . . Just throwing this out there, but what would you say to me calling downstairs and booking this room for another night?"

Grayson's face lights up like the Fourth of July. "*What would I say?*" He sits up, grips my face in his palms, and plants an enthusiastic kiss on my mouth that makes me gasp and laugh. "I'd say, 'Fuck yes, let's do it! And then I'd say, 'Thank you, Selena, and thank you, Baby Jesus, for giving me another night with this perfectly pulchritudinous goddess!'"

6

GRAYSON

"Sorry I'm late," I say to Max, sliding into a chair across from him at the sushi restaurant he's picked for our lunch.

It's Sunday afternoon. About an hour since I said a heartbreaking goodbye to Selena at the hotel. I tried and failed to get her to put a dinner date on the calendar for this coming week. Thankfully, she at least said she'd think about it and let me know, rather than totally shutting me down. But as it stands now, I have no idea if I'll ever see Selena Diaz again. It's a tough pill to swallow, considering how much fun we had together, and how my heart is already feeling for her. But given the Boy Scout pledge I made to her on Friday night, I'm resolved to hang back this week and give her the space she needs.

"So, how'd it go on Friday night with Mrs. Robinson?" Max says.

"It was the best night of my fucking life."

Max's eyebrows shoot up.

"That is," I add, "until Saturday night rolled around and blew Friday out of the water."

Max's eyebrows ride up even higher. "You wound up spending *two* nights with her?"

I nod and grin like a Cheshire cat. "After we left Captain's on Friday, we went to a hotel and didn't leave until an hour ago. I left the hotel, went to my place for a quick change of clothes, and came straight here."

"Holy fucking shit, Grayson! How'd you convince her to spend all weekend with you?"

"It wasn't too hard. I'm a sex machine, man."

Max guffaws, obviously thinking I'm kidding. "Well, whatever you did, it worked. Are you gonna see her again tonight?"

I try to keep my voice neutral and calm. "I'm not sure when we'll hook up again. We're keeping things casual."

Max turns his head and gives me a hard side-eye. "She blew you off?"

"Not at all. She said she's gonna be really busy this week, so she'd let me know when she's free." I press my lips together. I've never been good at lying. "Yeah, I guess she sort of did."

"Oh, shit. What happened?"

"Nothing happened." I pick up a menu. "We both thought the whole weekend was amazing. She said so, a bunch of times. It's just that she's not looking for any kind of relationship, and she's convinced I am."

"Well, to be fair, she's not wrong."

"Yeah, but not with *her*. I'd take anything she'd give me. And I told her so."

Max looks deeply skeptical. "Dude, you're not even convincing *me*. I can't imagine you came close to convincing her."

I put the menu down and sigh. "I didn't. She could read me like a book."

"It's not hard to do." He looks sympathetic. "You really like her, huh?"

I nod. "I tried my best not to catch feelings for her. I swear I did. Over and over again, I said to myself, 'Be like Max. Be like Max!'"

He guffaws.

"She made it clear, right from the start, she has no room in her life for a boyfriend. And I told her that was fine with me. Let's go, baby!"

"Hell yeah."

"But as the weekend wore on, I could feel myself falling for her, no matter how hard I tried to keep myself in check. The thing is, our chemistry was fucking incredible—and not just physically, but, like, *spiritually*. The way I felt with her was a soul connection, man. Like, once-in-a-lifetime shit."

Max laughs. "Please, tell me you didn't say any of this to her."

"Of course, not."

"Please, tell me you managed to come off a whole lot cooler with her than you are right now."

I grimace. "That one, I can't be sure about."

He exhales. "So, how'd you leave it with her? I assume you put your heart in her hand and said, 'This is yours now.'"

"*No*. I just said, 'The ball is in your court.'"

"That's the same thing, coming from you. I'm sure your face said the rest."

"No, I think I'm okay. I was referring to something she'd said at Captain's. Before we headed out, she made me promise she wouldn't need to block my number or get a restraining order on me afterwards, and I accepted her terms and conditions."

Max processes that information for a moment. And then, "Okay, here's what you do. Let her come to *you* this week. If she doesn't, then send her flowers at the end of the week, which will prompt her to text *you* to say thanks, at which point you'll reply and ask her to dinner or drinks."

My heart rate is picking up speed. "Unfortunately, I have no idea where to send flowers."

"Where does she work?"

"I have no idea. We only talked a little bit about our jobs, in general. We skipped all the usual small talk and went straight to talking about—"

"I don't care what you talked about, Gray. Did she tell you her last name?"

I nod. "Diaz."

He grabs his phone off the table, a man on a mission. "Okay. Easy peasy. We'll find her on LinkedIn, you'll send her a jaw-dropping bouquet of flowers in four or five days, if you haven't heard from her, telling her you can't stop thinking about her and want to see her again, and she'll be putty in your hands."

"Oh, I like that idea. Selena never said I can't send her flowers. She only made me promise not to light up her phone!"

Max taps on his phone. "She spells Selena with two e's?"

"I think so. I didn't ask."

"Hmm. That's a common name." He taps a bit more. "Does she spell Diaz with a z or an s?"

"I don't know. I was assuming a 'z,' but I guess I could be wrong. Fuck."

Max twists his mouth, still tapping buttons on his phone. "Selena is sometimes spelled with an 'i' in the middle. There are a lot of Selena Diazes, with Selena spelled both ways."

"Shit."

"Are you gentlemen ready to order?" It's our waitress, appearing out of nowhere.

"Oh, sorry. I haven't looked at the menu yet," I admit.

She says that's fine and gets our drink orders before heading off.

"Do you think maybe Selena gave me a fake name?" I ask, my stomach twisting at the thought.

"Of course, not. Her friends all called her Selena, repeatedly, remember?"

"That's true. But maybe she told her friends to call her by a fake name, in case I turned out to be a creep."

"You're paranoid," Max declares.

"You'd be paranoid, too, if you'd been given as many fake numbers as me."

"That's nothing but a string of bad luck, Gray. When I was with her friend, Marnie, she said she'd met 'Selena' in college at U Dub. I can't imagine Marnie would have remembered to keep using a fake name for her, hours later, and after having several more drinks."

I pause. "Actually, come to think of it, the hotel clerk called her 'Ms. Diaz.'"

"See? Paranoid."

"So, did you wind up hooking up with Selena's friend on Friday night after you two went outside 'for a smoke'?"

Before Max answers my question, the waitress returns with our drinks. After we quickly scan our menus, she takes our food orders and leaves, at which point I lean forward and say, "Back to Friday night. Did you hook up with Selena's friend after Captain's?"

Max nods. "We went back to my place, and that woman was like a cougar on a fox." He snickers. "Cougars are always the most fun. They don't play coy or feel like they need to wait for a certain number of dates to bang you. If they're feeling chemistry, they go for it, no holds barred. No second-guessing themselves." He brings his fingers to his lips and makes a "chef's kiss" gesture.

"Nice! Maybe we could all go out to dinner together this week. That'd be a natural reason for me to text Selena!"

Max shrugs. "Meh. Sorry, Gray. I can't help you there. I'd hook up with Marnie again, if we bumped into each other or she texted me for a booty call. The sex was straight-up fire. But as far as going out to dinner with her, or asking her out on an actual date, I'm not feeling it."

I'm stupefied. From what I saw between the pair at the bar, their chemistry was strong. And he just said the sex was incredible. So, why wouldn't he want to try dating her? I swear to God, sometimes, Max's commitment to being non-committal annoys the hell out of me. I say, "It looked like you were having fun with her at the bar. Why not take her out to dinner and see if—"

"Nah. Sorry, Gray. I'd love to help you out, but I'm just not feeling it with her." He takes a languid sip of his drink, before adding, "Honestly, after the booze wore off, I found her kind of boring."

Damn.

Hearing Max talk in such blasé terms about Marnie, especially after witnessing what I *thought* was blazing-hot chemistry between the pair at Captain's, only emphasizes the amazingness of my night with Selena. Not only was the sex fire with her, but every conversation before and after was incredible, too. The furthest possible thing from "boring." In fact, I felt endlessly electrified in Selena's presence, all weekend long.

To distract myself from thoughts of Selena, I decide to switch topics and ask Max about a big patent case he's assigned to at work. And off he goes, telling me all about it. Even though I'm not a lawyer and only work in the IT department at the same firm with Max, it's apparently not a breach of his duty of confidentiality to talk to me, a fellow employee, about cases. Or at least, that's how Max has explained it to me.

"Interesting," I say, even though what he's telling me isn't all that interesting. Or maybe it is, but I'm too wrapped up in thoughts of Selena to give him a fair shake. When Selena and I said goodbye, should I have tried harder to get her to commit to a date with me, or did I do the right thing by being respectful of her stated boundaries, as promised? In the moment, I thought I was doing the right thing, but now I'm not sure if I made it clear enough how enthusiastically I want to see her again.

"Here you go," the waitress says, appearing with our food.

"Thanks," I say, as she puts my order in front of me. When she leaves, I grab my phone off the table. "If I can't send Selena flowers, then I should send her a quick little text, letting her know how much fun I had—"

"No, Grayson. Put the phone down."

"Just a little note to—"

"No. Trust me. Let her come to *you*."

"Too late. I sent it."

"What?" Max blurts. "No!"

I shrug. "There's no point in me pretending to be someone I'm not. Yes, I promised not to bombard her with texts, but if I didn't send one little text today to say I had a blast with her this weekend and want to see her again, she'd wonder if I got murdered or hit by a bus."

"Grayson."

"It's okay. She knows I'm a total dork, Max. If I follow your advice and act like *you* would in this situation, I wouldn't be the guy she wanted to spend the night with, in the first place."

He makes a face that concedes I've got a point. "So, what'd you say in your text?"

I hand my phone to him, and he cringes sharply when he reads my message.

"What the fuck is *pulchritudinous*?"

"It means beautiful."

"She's not gonna know that!"

"Actually, she will, because I called her that several times this weekend."

Max grimaces with disgust. "You're such a fucking weirdo, Grayson."

"You're not wrong. Lucky for me, however, Selena apparently likes weirdos. At least, this weirdo. Because it was only *after* I called her a 'perfectly *pulchritudinous* goddess' that she invited me to stay with her a *second* night."

Max snorts.

"Plus, not to make you feel bad or anything, but I seem to recall you hitting on Selena, pretty hard, before I got to our table at Captain's. And yet, she wanted to leave with a weirdo like *me*. Go figure."

Max chuckles. "Touché. In my defense, though, you had a pretty big head start with her."

"That's true."

"Either way, I'd bet anything that dorky text won't move the needle with her, especially not this soon. Even if she wants to see you again, I'm betting she'll wait a few days to respond, if only to teach you the art of patience."

As Max is finishing his sentence, my phone pings. And when I look down, I contort my lips, trying to keep from smiling.

"You'd bet *anything*?" I ask. "What do you want to bet?"

"*No.*"

I waggle my eyebrows. "It seems Selena *really* likes dorky weirdos. Or at least, this one."

"What did she say?"

I can't keep my smile at bay a moment longer. "She wants to know if I'm available to meet her at the hotel again . . . *tonight!*"

7
SELENA

It's Sunday afternoon, and I'm sitting at my kitchen table, sipping a cup of herbal tea, while my beloved fur baby, Daisy, sleeps at my feet. Every muscle in my body is sore from this weekend's delicious fuckery with Grayson, my cheeks hurt from smiling and laughing so much, and my throat feels slightly raw from all those screams of ecstasy. Even if my brain knows it's for the best to put Grayson firmly in my rearview mirror and consider him nothing but a happy memory, my body won't stop reminding me of the incredible fun we had together this weekend.

If I hadn't known Drew would be returning home from his father's house at three today, I'm positive I would have thrown logic and caution to the wind and suggested Grayson and I spend yet another night together in that hotel room. But, alas, I did know it. So, I did the responsible thing. I kissed him goodbye, told him I'd had a fantastic weekend with him, and remained non-committal about any future plans. I figured I'd come to my senses and regain control of my raging hormones and fluttering heart, once I got home and back into the swing of my real life. I figured a little time apart from Grayson would harden my resolve not to lead him on. But in reality, this time away from Grayson has only made me ache to see that cutie again, as soon as possible.

I pick my phone up . . . but quickly put it back down. What would be the point in sending Grayson a text? The man is twenty-five and looks even younger than that. We'd look ridiculous together, out on a date! I think I look damned good for thirty-eight, but, still, I'm clearly much older than him. And I certainly don't want to be a hypocrite! How many times have I roasted Andre to my friends about him being a Peter Pan who never dates women his own age?

"Thanks, Dad!" I hear Drew calling out in the driveway, followed by the sound of a car door slamming shut. I walk toward the front door, eager to greet my son, and, of course, my movement awakens Daisy and prompts her to shuffle toward the door alongside me.

"Hey, Mom!" Drew says brightly, after flying through the front door. He hugs me, and then our faithful pooch, and asks if there's anything to eat.

"Yeah, I picked up some food for you from the Greek place. I figured you'd be hungry."

"Thanks!"

We head into the kitchen together, and I get busy pulling the food I got for him out of the fridge.

"Did you have fun with your father?" I ask, taking care to keep my voice light and non-judgmental, as best I can. Since day one, I've been careful not to shit-talk Andre to Drew, even when my inner dialog was anything but kind. With the help of my brilliant therapist, I've realized it's vitally important not to make Drew ever feel like he has to pick sides between Andre and me. I've realized Andre only made those marriage vows to me. Yes, he was a shitty husband. A liar and cheater. Emotionally abusive and manipulative. But, perhaps, over time, he could partly make that up to me by becoming a better father to our son.

"The weekend was fine," Drew says. He takes a seat at our kitchen table. "I barely saw Dad, though. He was too busy with his new girlfriend to pay much attention to me. But Kellan came over from across the street and we played video games all weekend, so that was cool."

I force myself not to scoff too loudly. "Here you go. I got extra tzatziki sauce for you."

"Thanks." He digs right in. "So, what'd you do this weekend?"

"I went out for drinks with Victoria and a few others on Friday night, which was fun. And other than that, I worked out and relaxed." It's all technically true. Granted, my "workout" consisted of having more orgasms in a two-day span than I've ever had in my life. And when I "relaxed," it was naked in bed with Grayson. But, hey, not a false word was spoken.

"You want to watch a movie tonight?" I ask, after watching Drew chowing down happily for a long moment. "I'm even willing to watch one of your horror movies, if it'll convince you to hang out with me."

"Can't," he says. "Sorry. I've got to do a big group project with Eddie tonight."

"When's it due?"

"Tomorrow."

"*Drew*."

"It's not my fault, Mom. The other two people in the group had to do their parts before Eddie and I can do ours, and they only just finished an hour ago." He flashes me his dimpled smile —the one he knows melts me the most. "Eddie invited me to spend the night tonight, so we can work all night, if needed. Can I go? His mom already said yes, as long as it's okay with you."

My heart lurches with excitement, but I try to keep my face impassive and unreadable. But it's a lucky break! Every fiber of my body wanted to book that hotel room with Grayson for a third night! And now, if he's game, I can do exactly that!

"Eddie's mom said she'd drive us to school tomorrow morning," Drew says, obviously interpreting my excited silence as a "no."

"I don't like sleepovers on school nights," I say, simply because that's what I'd normally say in this scenario, if I weren't chomping at the bit to shag a certain twenty-five-year-old again.

"I know, but this is for school, Mom. We might have to stay up really late tonight, working."

"Will you promise to get to sleep no later than eleven?"

"How about midnight, just in case the project takes that long?"

"Okay. Deal."

His face bursting with excitement, Drew gets up and kisses my cheek, like he's won a major concession from me. So, I pat his back and let him think it.

"Can you drive me to Eddie's, or should I ride my bike?"

"I'll take you, so you don't have to leave your bike over there tomorrow morning."

"Oh, yeah. Thanks, Mom."

"Go get your stuff. We'll leave now, so you have as much time as possible to work on your project."

"Awesome! Thanks again!" And off he goes upstairs, with our dog, Daisy, traipsing happily behind him.

I watch Drew and Daisy disappear up the stairs, and the second they're out of sight, I breathlessly pick up my phone to text Grayson about my unexpected availability tonight. But to my surprise, my phone pings as I'm lifting it with a new text from Grayson!

> Grayson: Sorry if I'm sending this text way too soon in violation of my promise to you, but my thirst to behold your pulchritude must be slaked! When can I see you again, goddess? Tell me when I can take you to dinner!

> Me: I'm unexpectedly free tonight. Are you available? We could do another sleepover at the hotel and dine in our room after FUCKING LIKE ANIMALS.

> Grayson: OMFG! YASSS!

I can't help giggling at the string of celebratory emojis he's added to his message.

> Me: Woohoo! I'll head over to the hotel now and text you the room number when I have it. Maybe we'll get lucky, and they'll still have our room available.

> Grayson: Selena, I'd be happy with you in a broom closet. See you soon.

I send him a dancing-woman emoji, and he replies with another string of celebratory emojis.

"Who are you texting?" Drew asks. He's coming down the staircase, a backpack slung over his shoulder.

I look up. "Huh?"

"Who are you texting? You're smiling really big. Is that Victoria?"

"Mm hmm. Come on, honey. Let's get you to Eddie's. Did you pack your pills and retainer?"

"Pills, yes. Retainer, no. I'll get it." He shuffles away, like he has all the time in the world, so I use the time to quickly run to my room to gather a change of clothes and toiletries. Before leaving my room, I text my neighbor to ask about their teenage daughter caring for Daisy tonight, as usual when I'm away, and then, I race down the stairs, assuming Drew will be down there, waiting for me. But, shit, he's not.

"Drew!" I call up the stairs. "Come on!"

"In a minute!" he yells.

"Whatever you're doing, it can wait!" I yell. "Let's go!"

Finally, he clomps down the stairs. But he's not carrying his backpack.

"Backpack?" I shout.

"Oh. Whoops. Left it upstairs."

"Don't forget your retainer!"

"Oh yeah."

I roll my eyes. The boy would lose his head, if it wasn't attached to his neck.

Finally, Drew appears again, this time with his backpack slung over his shoulder.

"You have your pills and retainer?" I ask. It's the same question I ask literally every time he's headed out the door to his father's house or anywhere else for the night.

"Yup."

"Wonderful." My heart racing, I grab my keys off the counter and begin striding with my small overnight bag toward the front door.

"Oh, wait. I want to grab some snacks," Drew says. "There's never anything good to eat at Eddie's house."

Good lord, I'm going to explode, if I don't get to that hotel and into Grayson's arms as soon as possible. Every minute that's passed since I said goodbye to Grayson has only made me crave seeing him again, all the more.

"I'll give you money to order a pizza!" I blurt, my voice sounding weirdly excited and strained. I clear my throat. "Or you and Eddie can walk to the minimart down the block and buy whatever you want." Hastily, I grab my purse and shove some bills at my son, who suddenly looks awfully suspicious of me. "Here. Knock yourself out."

Drew narrows his eyes as he takes the cash. "Are you in some kind of hurry, Mom?" His eyes drift to the bag I'm holding. "Are you going somewhere?"

"No." I indicate the bag. "This is dry cleaning. Now, come on." I turn and stride toward the front door, praying Drew is following me. "Your project is due tomorrow, remember? That means every minute counts!"

8

GRAYSON

"Hello, handsome," Selena says, waggling her eyebrows suggestively.

"Hello, goddess." I lean into the doorway of the hotel room for a little peck. "Damn, I missed the sight of you."

Selena giggles. "It's been a couple hours."

"I know. *Torture*."

With that, I walk past her into our latest hotel suite, and Selena gives my ass a playful little thwap as I go. The minute we're both in the room and the door has closed behind her, she throws her arms around my neck, and I pull her into me and crush my hungry lips against hers. We kiss passionately for a long, heated moment, the heat between us like two long-lost lovers reunited after war.

Just this fast, my cock is already rock-hard, not surprisingly. This woman does crazy things to me. So, I back her toward the bed, still kissing her, and sit her down on the edge of the mattress. From the moment I left Selena earlier today, I've been craving the taste of her, the scent of her, the sounds of her moans, like a junkie in need of a fix. And now that I'm here, I want all of it, right fucking now.

I kneel, slide the hem of her dress up, and pull her panties off. But right before dropping them on the ground next to me, I have the sudden impulse to slide them into the pocket of my jeans. So, that's exactly what I do, my eyes locked with hers.

"Naughty boy," she whispers. But it's clear from her expression, she likes naughty boys. Or at least, she likes this one.

My trophy stowed in my pocket, I slide my fingertips up and down her slit, making her yearn for more. And when she begins shuddering visibly with arousal, I widen her thighs, take a nice long inhale of her intoxicating scent, and then dive voraciously into my meal, groaning along with her as she loses herself to pleasure.

As my mouth continues its enthusiastic assault on Selena's pussy, my fingers slide inside her—and her appreciative moan spurs me on like wild, instantly sending pre-cum dripping from my tip. As the intensity of our mutual pleasure rises, she grips my hair fiercely and gasps out a string of curse words, and two seconds later, her most intimate muscles ripple against my fingers, tongue, and lips.

With my breathing erratic and my heart pounding like a jackhammer, I pull out my throbbing, straining cock and quickly get my length covered with a condom from my wallet, as Selena lies before me on the bed, still half-dressed, writhing and pleading with me to fuck her. I should probably rip her clothes off, and then mine, but I'm too turned on to wait a single unnecessary second to get inside her.

As my entire body thrums with lust, I turn her over on the bed, guide her onto her hands and knees, and bite her ass, hard. "This gorgeous ass is *mine*," I declare, before grabbing her hips and plunging myself inside her.

For a split-second, I think, "Shit, I probably shouldn't have called her ass *mine*, in case she thinks *I* think we're exclusive." But thank God, the thought is immediately obliterated from my mind as Selena begins screaming she's gonna come.

"Don't stop!" she shrieks. "Don't change anything! I'm gonna come so hard! Oh, God, baby! Don't ever stop!"

It's one of my favorite things about fucking this woman—how vocal and uninhibited she is about what works for her. I love that she takes the guesswork out of making her come by shamelessly going after what feels good for her, which thereby only helps me get her there so much faster and harder.

Hearing Selena's screams of ecstasy while looking at the angry red mark I've just left on her ass cheek takes me to the bitter cusp of losing it. But, somehow, I manage to keep thrusting energetically, willing myself to hang on until she gets where she's going.

Just when I think I'm a goner, that I can't hang on a second longer, Selena finally reaches climax. After releasing a desperate whimper, followed by a long, animalistic groan, Selena's innermost muscles surrounding my cock begin rippling and squeezing me, which instantly slingshots my pleasure straight into the fucking stratosphere.

As bliss consumes me, my eyes roll back and my vision blurs like I'm overdosing on an illicit drug. Still in the throes of pleasure, I feel Selena's body collapsing underneath mine onto the mattress, so I fall on top of her, incapable of holding myself up through my release.

When I'm capable of commanding my limbs again, I slide off Selena and onto my back, which allows her to flip onto her back next to me.

"I knew you couldn't resist another round with a sex god like me for long," I tease.

"I'm only human, after all."

"So you say. Not sure I believe that, though. I think you're supernatural."

Selena giggles. "Want to know a secret? When you texted me, I was literally just about to text you."

I turn my head to smile at her. "What? And risk me blocking your number?"

She bites her lip. "I like to live dangerously."

Before I can reply to that, Selena's phone pings on the nightstand, and she turns to grab it, murmuring, "It might be Drew." She looks at her screen and snorts loudly, before tapping out a quick reply and returning the phone to its original spot on the nightstand. She smiles and says, "So, are you hungry?"

"Was that your son?" I ask. I realize it's none of my business, but I'm intrigued by her obvious amusement.

"No, it was my friend, Lucy. The one with the red hair? Her daughter, Kelsey, works as a hostess at The Turnpike. You know that restaurant on 5th?"

I shake my head.

"It's really good. Anyway, Kelsey texted her mom a photo of a certain couple who just got seated, so Lucy texted the photo to *me*." Selena snickers. "Apparently, my ex is dining with a blonde tonight who barely looks old enough to drink." She rolls her eyes. "I swear, the man's got an addiction." She waves her manicured hand. "It doesn't matter. He's not my problem anymore."

"Let's go!" I blurt.

"Where?"

"To the restaurant! Let's let your ex see he's not the only one dating someone young and hot as fuck!"

Selena snorts. "Thanks, but as hot as you are, I truly don't give a shit about him. I certainly don't want to waste our valuable time and your hotness trying to piss him off. I want you all to myself."

I pull a face registering my disbelief. "You're sincerely telling me it wouldn't feel fucking amazing to see his face when he realizes you've been getting railed by a much younger, hotter dude with a much bigger cock, who fucking *loves* eating your pussy?"

She giggles. "Well, damn, when you put it like that . . ."

"Come on, Selena! It'll be fun!"

She twists her mouth, considering my proposal.

"Think of this as a favor to *me*!" I insist. "I'd *love* to see this prick's arrogant face when he realizes what's good for the gander is good for the goose—especially when the goose is the goddess he treated like fucking shit!"

Selena knits her brows together. "Only if you're positive you wouldn't feel, I dunno, used and abused by me doing this. You're not some kind of trophy boy toy to me, Grayson. You know that, right?"

I laugh. "What do you mean I'm not your trophy boy toy? How dare you!"

She laughs. "You're so funny, Grayson. Okay, let's do it."

I fist-pump the air. "Woohoo!"

"But let's not eat a meal there. I don't want to be around him that long. We'll go to the bar area in the back to have a cocktail, and then leave and go somewhere else for dinner."

"Love it."

"I truly don't need or want his approval or opinion about a goddamned thing anymore. I've moved on. I want to make it clear I'm doing this solely for our entertainment value—so we can laugh about it together, later on, after you've 'railed' me, brilliantly, for the umpteenth time."

"Sounds fucking awesome to me. Although, come on, nobody ever 'moves on' enough from their cheating, lying, douchebag of an ex to the point where they wouldn't appreciate them knowing they're having much hotter sex with the next guy."

Selena snickers. "Well, that's true."

"But I get what you're saying and I'm down to do this, for entertainment value, if nothing else." I take her hand and kiss it enthusiastically, and then leap off the bed like a man possessed. "Come on, baby. Pull your dress down, muss your hair a little so it looks like you just got fucked, and take your trophy boy toy out for a drink!"

Selena stands, runs her fingers through her thick, dark hair, and extends her palm to me. "My undies, please."

I shake my head. "Nope. They're mine now."

"*What?*"

I wink and grin. "It'll be extra hot for both of us to know your pussy is secretly bare under there, as we sit at the bar, enjoying a cocktail mere feet away from your ex, knowing the whole time that controlling bastard is losing his goddamned fucking mind."

9
GRAYSON

After parking my car down the block from the restaurant, I jog around the back bumper to open the passenger door for Selena. Before exiting the car, she flips up the hem of her dress and briefly flashes me a quick but delightful glimpse of her panty-less pussy, before taking my offered hand and exiting from the car like the Queen of England arriving at a royal engagement.

"That was hot," I mutter. "*Thank you.*"

Laughing, Selena comes to a stand next to me on the sidewalk and bats her eyelashes playfully. "What can I say? I'm a freak in the sheets and a lady in the streets."

"You're the gold standard for that particular expression, as a matter of fact. How am I going to walk on *three* legs the full block to the restaurant?"

She giggles. "Soldier on, young buck. I have faith in you."

"That was so fucking sexy," I mutter, entwining my fingers in hers. "You're incredible, Selena."

Our hands intertwined, we begin walking the short distance to the restaurant. And even though I know it's silly, I can't help feeling like a fucking king to be seen out in public with her, holding her hand. To be able to walk down the sidewalk with this elegant, sensual, vivacious woman as my date, knowing everyone we pass can clearly see she's picked *me*, out of all the men in the world, at least for tonight.

When we reach our destination, there appears to be a long wait for a table, based on the large, scattered crowd milling about.

"This place is a real hot spot, eh?" I observe.

Selena rolls her eyes. "Andre would never deign to dine at a cute little hole-in-the-wall." She peeks through a window of the restaurant. "He's here. His back is facing us, but I'd know that head anywhere."

A wave of excitement ripples through me. "You're still good to do this?"

Selena returns from the window to smile wickedly at me. "Actually, now that we're here, I must admit I'm chomping at the bit to see the look on his face when he sees me with you."

"Same. Let's make it *really* clear we're not merely friends."

"Absolutely."

After stealing a quick kiss, I open the door for Selena, and we head inside the packed restaurant. When the hostess greets us, Selena hugs her, introduces her to me as Kelsey, her good friend's daughter, and lets the young woman know we won't be needing a table tonight, that we're headed back to the bar for a cocktail. The woman asks Selena if she's aware her ex is already dining here, and Selena says, "Yes, your mom sent me the photo. We're going to walk past him on our way to the bar and have a little fun with him." With that, she grabs my hand again and leads me into the crowded restaurant.

As we walk, Selena leans into me and whispers, "See the blonde with the big boobs over there?" She juts her chin at a far corner table. "That's him sitting across from her."

I look to where Selena has indicated and quickly spot our mark—a guy in a black shirt with broad shoulders and salt-and-pepper hair, who's sitting across from a young blonde with noticeably large breasts.

"Even the back of his head looks douchey," I whisper, making Selena laugh. But I can't help noticing, just this fast, the guy seems like a force to be reckoned with. Even from the back, it's clear he's got a pretty muscular frame, far more muscular than mine. But not only that, even from behind, he's got an unmistakably commanding presence. "Okay, baby," I say, squeezing her hand. "Let's turn up the heat as we walk by—make it look like we just got finished fucking before arriving here and can't wait to do it again."

"Which is true," she murmurs.

She drops my hand, snakes her arm around my waist, and snuggles close, so I slide my palm squarely onto her glorious ass cheek.

"Okay if I grope your ass noticeably as we walk by?" I whisper.

"Please do," she whispers back. "And say my name. *Loudly.*"

Right on cue, as we're passing the douchebag's head, I squeeze Selena's ass with my full palm in a way I'd never normally do in public, especially not in a hoity-toity restaurant like this, and say, much too loudly, "Damn, *Selena*, I can't wait to get back to the hotel and rail you again."

Selena, on my left, turns her head to smile wickedly at me, presumably giving her ex to my right a fantastic view of her face.

"Selena," a deep male voice blurts, and she comes to a sudden stop, halting me along with her.

"Andre?" she says, sounding impressively surprised. So, of course, I take the opportunity to peek at the asshole.

No.

Oh, God, no.

Fuck.

Selena's douchebag ex is Andre De La Torre! *My motherfucking boss.* And by "boss," I don't mean he's my *immediate* supervisor in the IT department at the law firm where I work. I don't mean he's my boss's boss, either. No, the man currently staring at me with hard, murderous eyes is *everyone's* fucking boss at my employer— which, by the way, is called Finch, Gardner & *De La Torre.* He's the managing partner and co-founder of the firm, a guy whose last name is literally engraved in marble above the goddamned door.

And even worse than all that, Andre De La Torre *personally* oversees operations at the firm, including overseeing all employees, both legal and non-legal, including lowly minions like me in the IT department, including overseeing all hiring, firing, and promotions, all of which ultimately require the big boss's stamp of approval.

I can't believe this is happening! I interviewed with Andre De La Torre just this past week in his sleek corner office, as the last hurdle in my quest to nab that coveted promotion! Which means, unless this man's got some sort of facial amnesia or another neurological disorder, he's currently recognizing me as the lowly IT guy who's gunning for a big promotion at his law firm, every bit as much as I'm recognizing him as the man who signs my paychecks and holds my current career aspirations in the palm of his hand.

"You were so lucky to get a table tonight—especially such a cozy one!" Selena is saying, as Andre's laser-like, dark eyes burn holes into my eye sockets. "Grayson and I are only grabbing drinks in the bar. Oh, Andre, this is my boyfriend, Grayson—"

"McKnight," Andre interjects, his jaw tight.

Selena looks at me, her dark eyes wide. "*You know Andre*?"

"He works for me," Andre says, his voice steely.

"No, I *used* to work for you," I say, sounding far calmer than I feel. "Consider this my official resignation, *asshole.*"

"Grayson!" Selena gasps out, her body wobbling against mine. "No!"

"Consider this your immediate termination, *asshole*," Andre fires back.

I slide my arm around Selena's shoulders to steady her, not breaking eye contact with the man who clearly wants to slide his large hands around my neck. "Selena's told me all about you, and I have zero desire to work for a lying, cheating scumbag."

"Oh shit, let's go," Selena mutters, tugging on my arm, as her ex rises from the table, shouting a string of expletives.

"Not here!" a waiter shouts, appearing out of nowhere to fill the space between Andre and me.

"This woman is a fucking queen," I shout at Andre, as the waiter pushes me backward. "The fact that you cheated on her tells me everything I need to know about you." As the waiter drags me back, I shout to the young blonde at the table, who currently looks like a deer in headlights. "If you're dating him for his money, you're gonna earn every penny, sweetheart!"

Selena can't help chortling at that.

"Sir, *please*," the waiter says, as a big guy wearing a kitchen apron arrives to block Andre's progress toward me.

"I'm leaving," I say not only to the waiter pulling on my arm, but to all the wide-eyed diners staring at me in shock. "I've lost my appetite, anyway." I check to see if Andre is still within earshot, and when it's clear he is and I've got his full attention, I wet my lips suggestively with my tongue, wink at the asshole, and add, "For *food*, that is." With that, I take Selena's hand and pull her toward the front door like a Viking pillaging a small village, before glancing over my shoulder, one last time, to ensure Andre isn't about to tackle me from behind. Thankfully, that big guy in an apron seems to have Andre under control, though he looks fit to be tied, so I kiss the top of Selena's hand and lead her through the door.

As we step outside into the cool Seattle night, my skin barely registers the change in temperature, thanks to the massive amounts of adrenaline rushing through my veins. "Did you see his face at the end, when I made it clear I wanted to eat your pussy?" I say, laughing. "If that big guy wasn't there, I swear he would have murdered me!"

To my surprise, Selena doesn't laugh along with me, but instead looks distraught. "I'm so sorry about your job," she says. "I had no idea you worked for Andre! You only said you work in IT."

"Yeah, at his law firm, it turns out." I take her hand again and we begin walking down the sidewalk toward my parked car. "Your last name is Diaz? Not De La Torre?"

"I went back to using my maiden name after the divorce."

I can't help chuckling at the crazy set of circumstances that led us to this moment. "Can you imagine if, at Captain's, you'd said, 'Hi, my name is Selena De La Torre!' and I asked, 'Any relation to Andre De La Torre'?"

"If the conversation had gone that way, you'd still have a job."

"As far as I'm concerned, I got lucky I never found out the connection. If I had, it wouldn't have stopped me, by the way. I just might not have suggested coming down here tonight." I laugh again at the crazy coincidence.

"But your job, Grayson," she says, still looking distraught. "You've got rent to pay! A car payment!"

"I'll be fine. I meant what I said: I'd never want to work for a douchebag like him. This is a good thing."

She gasps. "The promotion! The condo you've been saving to buy!"

I squeeze her hand. "Stop, Selena. I'll be fine. I don't need to buy a condo, any time soon. Honestly, this is for the best. It's exactly the push I needed to do something I should have done a long time ago."

It's the truth. Now that I think about it, I only started saving for a condo because that's what Audrey wanted. But now that I'm single and can do whatever the fuck I want, why not use my savings to finally bet on myself?

"What do you mean?" Selena asks.

"There's this cool programing idea I've had for a long time. But I've always known I'd need to work on it full-time, probably for close to a year, to develop and test it. Before now, I could never figure out how to carve out enough time and money for me to go for it, so I put it on the back burner. But now, thanks to a lucky twist of fate, I've suddenly got all the time in the world and some money in the bank!"

We've arrived at my car now, so I open the passenger door for Selena before jogging around the back bumper to the driver's side. Despite what I just now said to Selena, I admit I feel a bit anxious about my sudden lack of employment. I've never quit a job without notice or having another job lined up.

But with each loping step I take around my car, my nerves calm down and certainty solidifies that tonight's crazy events were a blessing disguised as a curse. Now that I'm single, why on earth would I want to saddle myself with a mortgage? I'd much rather use that money to invest in myself. Even if I'm ultimately unsuccessful—if I run out of money before my app is completed—or if my completed app turns out to be a total failure—at least I won't have to go through the rest of my life, wondering, "What if?"

I settle into my driver's seat, latch my safety belt, and wink at Selena. "Don't worry about me, okay? This is gonna be great."

She smiles tentatively but says nothing, so I pull my car away from the curb.

After a brief moment of silence between us, Selena says softly, "Thank you for telling Andre I'm a queen. That meant the world to me."

I glance away from the road, briefly, to smile at her. "Just speaking the truth. It's honestly unethical how gorgeous you are."

Selena's tentative smile turns bright and wide as her shoulders soften. "Will you tell me about your app? I won't breathe a word about it to anyone, if your idea is confidential."

"Of course, I'll tell you. It's highly confidential, but I trust you completely."

"I trust you, too," she whispers, sending goosebumps across my flesh. "Completely."

We share a long, lingering smile. One that sends my heart thumping. But after a moment, I return to the road and say, "So, basically, my idea is a data-tagging mechanism to optimize artificial intelligence systems. I think over time it could transform any industry that relies on data collection. But I think, in the short-term, I could use the basic technology to get a cool app off the ground that makes online reservations for just about anything. And if that app is successful, then I think I could use that revenue expand my programming into a bunch of different industries."

"Wow," Selena says. "That sounds amazing. Explain the app to me in detail, if you would. Explain it to me like I'm a kindergartner."

For the next ten minutes of our drive, I tell her everything I can think of, breaking it down as simplistically as I can. And to my surprise, Selena asks tons of insightful, interesting questions that help me consider things in new ways. In particular, some of Selena's questions and comments make me realize there are even more potential uses and applications for my idea than I've been contemplating. Things I could do with my initial app idea, relatively quickly and easily.

"Thanks so much for talking this through with me," I say, as I turn my car into the hotel parking lot. "I was already excited to dive into the development process, in earnest, but now I'm chomping at the bit."

"I think you should launch an entire company from the outset," Selena says. "And make it clear the app is your opening salvo—your launching product—but there will be lots more to come. Make it clear to investors what else is coming down the line."

I snicker. "Investors?"

"Of course. An idea this big will need investors, Grayson."

I say nothing. Attracting investors to fund a start-up is a notoriously difficult thing to do. And getting to the sweeping level of success Selena is envisioning for my idea would require years, a full staff, and an insane amount of funding—far more than what's sitting in my bank account—not to mention a whole lot of business expertise I don't currently possess. But there's no reason to point any of that out to Selena, who's only trying to be supportive and cheer me on. So, I say, "Yeah, thanks. I'll certainly look into that."

After I've parked the car, we begin walking toward the hotel, each of us apparently lost in our own thoughts for a moment.

But finally, Selena says, "Would you be okay with me telling my best friend, Victoria, about your app idea? Remember her from Captain's? The one with the blonde bob. Victoria's the head of a prominent venture capitalist firm downtown, and—"

"*What?*"

"Yeah. She's always looking for start-ups and products to invest in! Victoria's been wildly successful at spotting diamonds in the rough—that's what she's most known for!"

"Holy fucking shit, Selena! Of course, I'd be stoked for you to tell Victoria about my app idea. Thank you."

"Fabulous. I'll call her on speaker phone the minute we get up to our room, and you can knock her socks off with everything you just told me in the car."

I palm my forehead. "You honestly wouldn't mind doing this for me?"

"Of course, not. Your idea is amazing. I mean, what I can

understand of it." She chuckles. "And, anyway, it's the least I can do, seeing as how you lost your job tonight because of me."

"Please, don't say that, Selena. I have zero regrets about tonight. Like I said, this is the shove I needed to pull my head out of my ass and take a chance on myself. As excited as I am, though, I can't let you call in a favor with your best friend because you wrongly think you owe me something. You truly don't."

Selena waves me off. "The only favor I could possibly call in with Victoria in a business situation is that she'll definitely take my call and hear you out. But that's it. Once you're on the call with her, you're on your own, kid. I can't help you anymore."

"I'm good with that. Let me at her."

Selena giggles. "Fair warning, Victoria mostly throws her weight behind female-led start-ups. But not always. She makes exceptions for the right projects."

"Hey, I'm just pumped to get the opportunity to make my pitch."

We enter the elevator in the hotel lobby, and I immediately grab Selena and kiss her passionately as the doors close.

"Thank you so much," I say. "You're an angel, sent from heaven."

"No, thank *you*," Selena whispers into my lips. "You made me feel like a queen tonight—like the most beautiful, *pulchritudinous* goddess in the world. Tonight, Grayson McKnight, you truly were my knight in shining armor."

10
SELENA

"A meeting tomorrow at ten o'clock works great for me!" Grayson replies to my best friend on speaker phone. "Thank you so much for the opportunity, Victoria."

"My pleasure," Victoria says. "I'm looking forward to my team hearing your pitch."

We wrap up the call and not two seconds later, Grayson is tackling me on the hotel bed, making me squeal and laugh at his exuberance.

"That went so well," I say, as he grinds his hard-on between my legs and peppers my face with frenetic kisses.

"You're an angel," Grayson coos. "Heaven sent."

He rips off his clothes, pins my arms above my head and yanks my dress up, revealing the naughty nakedness I've been hiding all night. As our lips consume and our tongues dance and swirl, he slides his fingers inside my wetness and presses his thumb against my clit, sending me higher and higher toward sheer bliss.

As he kisses and touches me, memories of everything that happened at the restaurant flicker across my mind. Everything

Grayson said and did was perfect. Sexy. *Alpha.* In the moment, I was scared for Grayson's physical safety and worried for his job. But I can't deny, even as I was scared and worried, a piece of me felt turned on to see him rise to the occasion and protect me like that. I felt insanely attracted to him in that moment, like a switch had flipped inside me and I wanted Grayson more than I wanted to breathe.

The murderous look on Andre's face, when he realized this young buck eats my pussy like he never did, definitely added fuel to my fire. What a deliciously satisfying moment that was for me, after all the times Andre cheated on me, and tried to gaslight me into thinking his cheating was *my* fault because I wasn't sexy enough, not sexual enough, not thin enough. And now, I've got a man who wants me, exactly as I am. Who's willing to shout to the entire world about his attraction to me. To defend my honor in front of Andre and the world and then take me back to our bed and fuck me good and right.

I come hard, arching my back and crying out with pleasure as I do, which turns Grayson into a shaking, panting mess.

"Oh, God, baby," he grits out, his entire body shuddering with extreme desire. Groaning, he firmly lodges his thick tip at my entrance, and leaves it there, teasing me, while we kiss passionately, and I grip his ass and push, nonverbally begging this hunky man to get himself inside me.

Normally, I wouldn't engage in sex without a condom with a new partner. But now that I know I'm only the second woman Grayson's been with, and that the last one was six months ago, I feel pretty damned safe to throw caution—and condoms—to the wind.

I rock my pelvis into his cock, and his tip enters me, making me moan. "Go ahead," I gasp out. "I've got an IUD. *Fuck me.*"

He doesn't need to be asked twice. With a husky growl, Grayson impales me, eliciting a loud moan from me as his cock burrows deep inside me.

We fuck passionately, until we're both grunting and groaning and losing our minds. We're reveling in the sublime sensations caused by our bodies moving together, so perfectly. Especially now that there's not so much as a thin layer of latex between us.

As we're both barreling toward climax, Grayson surprises me by suddenly pulling off my dress, which has been bunched at my chest all this time, and then my bra. And when we're both naked, he lies behind me, cleaves his body to mine, and begins fucking me from behind. As his cock fills me, his fingers find my clit and expertly massage me in slow circles, sending me to bliss on a bullet train.

It doesn't take long before I find myself on the brink of pure ecstasy. For a moment, I hover on the edge of the cliff, teetering there in suspended animation. I scream for him not to stop. To *never* stop. To please, oh, God, keep doing exactly *this*.

And a moment later, I'm throttled by an intense orgasm emanating from my deepest core—a climax that squeezes and grips Grayson's cock inside me, until he's coming along with me, his groans of pleasure bouncing off the walls of our hotel suite.

When we've both quieted down, I turn around to face him with my cheek on a pillow.

"Thank you for everything you said and did at the restaurant. Maybe I shouldn't admit this, considering you lost your job and I'm very sorry about that, but everything you did, what you said about me being a queen, the way you put your arm across me at one point, like you were *physically* protecting me . . . Oh, God, Grayson, all of it was a *huge* turn-on for me."

"It was a huge turn-on for me, too. And like I said before, don't be sorry about my job. What happened tonight was meant to be. Even if I didn't have my app idea, I wouldn't want to keep working for the man who treated you like shit. No fucking way."

I touch his chestnut hair. "You're such a good person. You've got integrity. Kindness. A heart of gold. And I love the way you own your feelings, whatever they might be."

"I don't think I'm capable of hiding my feelings. Even when I try to be stoic and mysterious—and trust me, I've tried—I'm terrible at it."

I giggle. "I can't imagine you as 'stoic and mysterious.' You wouldn't be *you*."

We exchange a smile.

"Are you hungry?" I ask.

"I am. Do you want to go out?"

"No. I'd rather stay here with you, in this amazing, sexy, happy bubble, as long as humanly possible. Is that okay with you?"

"That's fucking fantastic."

We order some room service, which we're told will take an hour to arrive. So, while we're waiting for our food, we take a shower together, during which we kiss and touch and caress.

Once our food arrives, we sit at a little table and eat in fluffy white bathrobes and talk and laugh about the exciting drama that unfolded, so surprisingly, at the restaurant earlier. We laugh about the looks on everyone's faces, from Andre's, to his date's, to the waiter and other staff members, and even other diners in the restaurant who clearly couldn't believe the drama unfolding before their eyes.

We also talk about Grayson's exciting pitch meeting tomorrow, with me giving him some inside information about Victoria, and eventually regaling him with some stories from college. That topic leads to Grayson telling me some funny stories about him and *his* best friend from college—a guy named Dimitri whom he met when both of them worked as tutors for student athletes.

"Do you get to see Dimitri very often these days?" I ask.

"Yeah, I went to his wedding in LA last month."

"Oh, how wonderful. Do you like his wife?"

"I love her. She's super cool and perfect for him."

"That's lovely." I don't mean to say the words that pop out of my mouth next, but out they come. "I'd love to meet Dimitri and his wife one day."

Unbridled joy bursts across Grayson's handsome face, seeing as how I've just confirmed I want to see him again after tonight.

"I'd *love* that," he says, trying but failing to sound calm. "Maybe we could go down to LA for a weekend getaway, whenever Drew is at his father's."

"That sounds fun. Let's look at our calendars and figure it out soon."

Grayson visibly vibrates with excitement as he says, "Cool." He's trying, but failing, to play it cool. And I must admit I adore him even more for it.

After a bit more conversation, we head into the bathroom to brush our teeth and get ready for bed. Back in the bedroom, we crawl underneath the covers, hold each other close, and talk in the moonlight. Now that I've thrown the door wide open to a world for Grayson and me beyond these four walls, we begin talking excitedly about things we'd like to do together on potential dates.

I mention I've got tickets for an upcoming Mariners game, and Grayson says he'd love to join me. Grayson says he heard something about a traveling Van Gogh exhibit coming to Seattle and asks if I'd like to go with him. His invitation is particularly thoughtful, since I only mentioned briefly, way back during our initial conversation at Captain's, that I was an art history major in college. Grayson remembering my college major is so sweet, in fact, after accepting his museum invitation, I find myself inviting him to join me on my weekly long hike with Daisy on Wednesday afternoon. Not surprisingly, Grayson leaps at the chance, saying he'd absolutely love to meet my beloved dog, after hearing so much about her.

We kiss and caress, as a feeling of euphoria I never want to end envelops us. But when I glance at the clock, and see the late hour, I gasp.

"You should get some sleep, Grayson! You've got a huge meeting in the morning that could literally change your life."

Grayson scoffs. "I don't think my body is going to be able to fall asleep any time soon, sweetheart." He pulls up the sheet by way of explanation, and when I see his straining erection under there, I can't help chuckling.

"One of the advantages of dating a twenty-five-year-old," he says.

"Apparently."

So, that's it. We're officially "dating" now, and I couldn't be more thrilled about it.

We make love slowly this time. Languidly, with both of us kissing each other tenderly and whispering words of adoration and excitement into each other's ears. But even with the difference in tempo this time, our chemistry is still white-hot and undeniable. In fact, even more so, after this wildly romantic night we've shared.

When we're done making love, Grayson pulls me into him tightly, kisses the top of my head, and says, "I don't want to date anyone but you, Selena."

"I only want to date you, too," I admit without hesitation, and then smile as Grayson squeezes me even more tightly. "But, still, I need to take this extra slow, okay? I want to be exclusive with you, but at a snail's pace."

He nods. "I can do that. Just as long as I know you're all mine, and I'm all yours, then I can take this as slow as you need."

"Thank you. That means the world to me." I pause. "Andre not only cheated on me. He was emotionally abusive. Not physically, but he threatened it. *A lot.* I was constantly terrified of him, scared of what he might do, if I pissed him off."

"Oh, Selena." He squeezes me and kisses my head. "I'm so sorry you went through that. Nobody should ever have to feel terrified like that. Ever."

"I've been working on myself for years, trying to sort through and heal the traumas of living like that. And I'm proud to say I've learned so much about myself and gained a world of confidence about who I am and what I deserve. But I don't want to use a feel-good relationship with you as a Band-aid for the wounds I still need to heal on my own."

"Whatever you need, however I can be there for you, I'll do it. That's another great thing about dating a twenty-five-year-old. I've got all the time in the world."

I chuckle. "I didn't even know men like you existed. I would have thought a younger man would be *less* patient with me." I run my fingertip down his forearm. "You're what I've been waiting for, without realizing I was even waiting."

Grayson kisses me. "And you're the fantasy I didn't even know I had."

"Oh, come on. You said yourself you've always had a thing for 'Stacy's Mom.'"

Grayson chuckles. "True, but that fantasy was about getting to *fuck* Stacy's Mom. I never even thought to fantasize about *dating* Stacy's Mom. That's a whole other level of fantasy fulfillment."

We kiss to seal the deal we've just made, and my heart feels like it's going to explode out of my chest with joy. But I tell myself to slow down and be realistic. As amazing as this night with Grayson feels, my rational brain still knows it's unlikely our insane connection will survive for long outside the walls of this hotel room, when real life creeps in and the novelty of this unlikely pairing wears off.

"Is something wrong?" he whispers.

"No. Not at all.

"You sighed."

"That was a swoon."

He sighs with relief. "Oh, good."

"Get some sleep, honey. I want you well-rested for that meeting tomorrow." I kiss his cheek. "My darling, sweet mogul-to-be."

11
SELENA

Six months later

I slather my face with moisturizer, prepping for the foundation I'm about to apply.

I'm standing in my bathroom in a fluffy robe after blow-drying my hair, hurriedly getting ready for tonight's exciting date with Grayson. After months of hard work and dedication by Grayson and his small team of coders, all of it funded by Victoria's VC group, my boyfriend's app finally launched today, and the buzz and numbers are already exceeding projections. In celebration, we're dining at a fancy steakhouse downtown, along with everyone who was involved in bringing Grayson's app-baby to life.

My phone on my bathroom counter rings, and Grayson's beautiful smile and twinkling, green eyes appear on my screen. Surely, he's calling in response to the apologetic text I sent two minutes ago, letting him know I'm running late but hurrying to get ready.

"Helllooooo, baby!" I sing out in greeting on speaker phone. "Drew's game unexpectedly ran into overtime, but I'm moving as fast as I can!"

"Did he win?"

"No."

"Shoot."

"He's bummed, but, you know, that's life."

"How long till you're on the road?"

"Fifteen minutes, if I really bust a move."

"I tell you what. I'm still fifteen minutes away from the restaurant. Why don't I swing by and pick you up?"

I smirk. Grayson made his suggestion so casually, like this change of logistics would simply make the most sense. Which it probably would, actually. But I know not to trust that seemingly nonchalant tone of his. For months, Grayson has been angling to at least glimpse my house—and even more so, to finally get to spend the night here with me, rather than bringing me to his apartment after a dinner date or meeting me at our usual hotel.

"I can pick you up at the curb and not come in, if Drew is there," Grayson adds.

"Honey, my house is twenty minutes from the restaurant, in the opposite direction. It wouldn't make any sense for you to double-back and come here."

"And how would I know that?" he asks playfully. "After six months, shouldn't I at least know my girlfriend's home address, so I can send her flowers every week?"

"You don't need to send me flowers, sweetheart. I love seeing your gorgeous smile as you personally hand a bouquet of flowers to me."

"But wouldn't it be extra romantic for a delivery guy to show up at your doorstep with a huge bouquet and say, 'Selena Diaz? These beauties are for you from your not-so-secret admirer!'?"

I giggle and lean into the bathroom mirror to apply some

eyeshadow. "I can't imagine anything more romantic than seeing the look on your face when you personally hand me a bouquet. But thank you for the sweet thought."

Grayson flaps his lips together but says nothing. By now, my sweet boyfriend is used to losing this playful game of tug of war with me. True to his word, he's been patient and respectful about my slow pace from day one. But that doesn't mean he's kept silent, especially lately, about his mounting desire to take our relationship to the next level.

"Why do you want to see my house so badly?" I ask coyly, even though I know why.

"Because you're the crayons to my coloring book," he declares without hesitation.

I'm smiling so big, I have to stop applying my eyeshadow, or I'll screw it up. Grayson's been saying cute stuff like that for months—telling me he loves me, without saying the magic words. I'm assuming he doesn't want to scare me off or risk rejection by saying those three little words first, before he's absolutely positive I'll say them back. Or maybe he's hoping to coax me into saying them first.

Without a doubt, I've been feeling deep love for this sweetheart of a man for months now. I thank my lucky stars every day he sent me that wrong number text. But, still, I think saying the actual words to him, this soon, would feel like I'm making a commitment to Grayson I'm not yet ready to make. After only six months, how could anyone know if their relationship is truly built to last? Especially when I've got Drew to consider, not to mention Grayson's age.

I rarely think about our age gap these days. But when I do think about it, I remember the pivotal and transformative nature of a person's twenties. It's a decade, by design, of deep personal growth and self-discovery. Surely, over the coming years, as Grayson gets closer and closer to his thirties, he'll get to know himself in ways he can't fathom now. He'll realize what he wants most out of life. And I can't help worrying he'll decide he wants things I'm simply not able to give him.

"It's fantastic to hear you think we're such a perfect match," I reply, leaning back into the mirror. "Because, darling, I've thought for some time now you're the golf *ball* to my *hole*-in-one."

Grayson reacts most enthusiastically when I throw out "I love you" replacements that involve balls and/or holes. Bonus points if a ball or object is being inserted into a hole or opening. And this time is no exception: he's laughing like a hyena at my silly quip.

"That's fantastic news," he says, still chuckling. "Since you're the spaghetti to my meat*balls.*"

"Well, isn't that lovely," I reply. "Since you're the teabag to my mug of hot water." It's not one of my best efforts, since there's no explicit reference to a ball or hole. But at least, I've come up with an object being inserted into an opening, so it's still a respectable offering in our game. Either way, it's the best I could come up with this time, after hitting a grand slam with that golf-ball/hole-in-one analogy a moment ago.

Much to my surprise, Grayson laughs even more enthusiastically about the teabag comment, than he did about the hole-in-one.

"What are you trying to do to me, you little vixen?" he says through his guffawing. "You can't talk that dirty to me when I'm driving, babe, or I'm liable to crash my car as all the blood rushes from my brain to my dick."

I furrow my brow. "The *teabag* one was especially dirty? You mean the hole-in-one, right?"

Grayson laughs even harder. "You don't even know what you said, do you?"

I bristle. "Of course, I do. The teabag goes into the mug. It's self-explanatory."

"Oh my God."

"I'm just surprised you're laughing harder at the teabag thing than the hole-in-one. I think the hole-in-one was my funniest offering yet."

Grayson is absolutely howling with laughter now. "Stop, babe. Or I'm not going to be able to drive." He catches his breath and chokes out, "Google 'tea-bagging' and 'sex' right now. I'll wait."

With a scowl on my face, I grab my phone, google the words he's directed, and gasp out loud when the explanation appears on my screen. "How have I never heard the name of that sex act before?" I blurt.

"Because you were never a teenage boy who spent half his life on the internet. Chin up, though. Even if you've never heard the term 'tea-bagging' before, you've most definitely performed the act like a motherfucking champ."

"*Grayson McKnight.*"

Again, Grayson laughs uproariously. "This is so *you*. You're effortlessly hot as fuck, without even realizing it. Which is exactly why you're the cotton candy to my cotton*balls,* Selena Diaz. The bread to my impossibly hard *banana*. The pulchritudinous, blue sky to my *penis*-shaped cloud with a throbbing, wet tip."

I can't help laughing along with him. "And *I'm* the raunchy one? Holy hell, Grayson."

"What can I say, baby? You turn me on."

I sigh. "You're so much better at this game than me. I really need to keep a journal of ideas, so I can step it up next time."

"Hey, you're the one who casually dropped a reference to sucking my balls, not me."

"*Grayson McKnight.* Stop it! You're making me blush."

"No, I'm not. You're far too talented at sucking my balls not to be loud and proud of your mad skills."

"Hush." I lower my voice, even though my bathroom door is

shut and there's no way my son could possibly hear me, even if he happened to be walking past my bedroom at this very moment. "I admit I'm a freak in the sheets who thoroughly enjoys 'teabagging' her hunky man behind closed doors, but that doesn't mean I want to discuss it."

Grayson snorts. "Such a lady."

"*Yes, in the streets.* Don't pretend you don't know how this game is played. Now, stop making me blush for real, because I need to figure out where to apply fake blush to my cheeks."

I perform my task as Grayson continues chatting happily about how adorable and sexy I am. When I'm finished with my makeup, I grab my phone, take it off speaker, and walk into my bedroom, intending to quickly throw on the little black dress that's already laid out on my bed. For some reason, though, I freeze with the dress in my hands and survey my bedroom, trying to see it through Grayson's eyes.

I look at my immaculately hand-carved bedroom furniture, a stunning set I had imported from Italy after seeing it in a craftsman's showroom during a Tuscan vacation. I take in the sitting area in the corner that's appointed with lush armchairs and a roaring fireplace and surrounded by floor-to-ceiling windows featuring a spectacular view of Puget Sound. And once again, I feel anxious about showing Grayson this aspect of my life.

I fantasize often about inviting Grayson to my home, whenever Drew is at his father's. I ache to make love to Grayson in my own, comfy bed and make him breakfast in my gourmet kitchen the next morning. I'd love to watch Grayson playing fetch with Daisy in the backyard. I imagine myself snuggling with him on the couch downstairs while watching a movie or sipping cocktails with Grayson in my hot tub and then fucking him senseless in the warm water.

But what if finally relenting and inviting Grayson into my home would somehow throw our magical relationship off-kilter? I've heard all about Grayson's humble upbringing. How hard it was for his single mother to make ends meet. What if seeing the luxury and splendor of my home—the views, the home gym and wine cellar, the formal dining room and spare bedrooms converted into glamorous walk-in closets—would intimidate Grayson or make him feel insecure about his bank account? I don't want to risk ruining a good thing. Not when I've found the greatest happiness of my life with Grayson, exactly as things are right now.

Grayson exhales loudly, cutting through the long silence between us. "Sweetheart, I'm not asking to come over there to pressure you in any way. I'm only asking because I genuinely want to know everything about you."

As my heart pounds, I sit on the edge of my bed with the phone pressed against my ear. I open my mouth, aching to tell him okay, yes, he can come pick me up right now, but the words simply won't form.

"You still there?" Grayson asks.

"Yes. Sorry. I was . . . contemplating."

"I don't have to meet Drew yet," he says. "I fully respect that you want to wait for our one-year anniversary for that next step. But when Drew's not home, couldn't I come over, even if it's only to pick you up for a date?" He pauses, waiting for me to reply, and when I don't, he forges ahead, apparently sensing he's making headway. "Baby," Grayson says softly, "I'm dying to see how you've decorated your place. I want to see the framed photos and books on your shelves." His voice turns low and sexy. "I want to rifle through your underwear drawer—and maybe even your hamper—and steal your sexiest pair of panties to add to my paltry little collection."

I giggle. "You've already got a pair—the black, lace ones you stole that very first weekend."

"Yes, I know. They're my prized possession. Unfortunately, however, they lost their glorious scent a long time ago."

"*Grayson.*"

"What can I say? I'm an addict, baby. A junkie. Your panties are my favorite sensory aid, whenever I'm alone in bed and missing my hot girlfriend who never lets me come over to her house."

"Naughty boy," I whisper.

"Only with you." He pauses. "Okay, I'm at the restaurant now. Are you close to leaving?"

"Uh, sort of. Hang on. I'm gonna put you down." I put the phone on the bed and throw on my dress. But as I'm doing so, I think I hear my dog, Daisy, scratching at my closed bedroom door. So, once my dress is on, I quickly swing open the door . . . And that's when I discover, to my shock, the noise I heard wasn't made by Daisy, but, rather, by my darling son who's very obviously been eavesdropping on my conversation with Grayson.

"Drew!" I blurt, as he stumbles back. "Fuck!" I grab my phone off the bed. "Gotta go. I'll see you soon! Order me an extra-dirty vodka martini!"

"I know exactly how you like it, babe!" Grayson calls out, before I shout a quick thanks and disconnect the call. With my heart hammering, I race back to my doorway, where I find my nefarious and nosey son fleeing down the hallway.

"Andrew De La Torre!" I shout to his retreating back. "Stop!"

To his credit, Drew halts, exhales visibly, and turns around, every inch of his face reflecting his guilt.

Fuck, fuck, fuck. Did Drew overhear Grayson and me talking about tea-bagging in my bathroom, for the love of fuck? No, I don't think Drew could have heard a single word said behind that closed door, thank God, even with the call on speaker phone.

But what did Drew overhear later on in the bedroom, when I had my phone pressed against my ear? Did I say the word "panties" or was Grayson the only one? I'm fairly certain only *Grayson* said the actual word, while I teased Grayson that he "already had a pair." But what other kind of "pair" could I have been referring to, if not panties? Gloves? Pants? Shoes?

Fuck! I think I said something about Grayson having stolen "my black, lace ones." Damn! That sure enough put the word "pair" into context. Plus, I'm positive I called Grayson a "naughty boy" toward the end of the phone call—and in a highly suggestive tone—which almost certainly wouldn't have gone misunderstood by a fourteen-year-old boy with raging hormones.

"How long were you listening to my phone call?" I demand.

"I didn't."

"Don't lie to me."

Drew rolls his eyes. "I only listened for like two minutes, Mom. And it wasn't a big deal. I already know about your boyfriend. I've known about him for months."

"What?"

He nods. "Dad told me months ago he bumped into you on a date with your boyfriend."

My jaw nearly clanks onto the floor. Fucking hell. What the fuck did Andre say about that encounter to our son? I'm too mortified to ask Drew for any details. I'll save that question for Andre.

"But even if Dad hadn't told me," Drew continues, most likely reacting to the rage he's seeing on my face, "I would have figured it out for myself. You've been running into another room to take calls from someone for months now, which you never do if it's Victoria or Marnie or a client. And then, I can hear you giggling on the phone, but trying to stifle it, so I won't hear. And after you've hung up, you always come back with this goofy smile on your face."

I press my lips together, rendered speechless.

"And every time you get that same goofy grin on your face

while texting with someone," Drew continues, "I always ask who you're texting with, hoping you'll finally come clean with me about your boyfriend." He shoots me the same stern look I wear when I'm scolding him. "*But you never do.*"

My face feels hot. He's just been caught, eavesdropping outside my door, and he thinks he can chastise *me* for withholding information from him that's none of his business? Ha! I'll be damned if I'm going to let my child flip the script on me! Crossing my arms I say, "Why didn't you tell me you knew, all this time?"

"Because you obviously didn't want me to know. Also, because it's been hilarious watching you lie like a rug." Chuckling at my annoyed facial expression, Drew walks toward me. "The more important question, Mother Dear, is why you've been hiding this guy from me? Do you think you're a bad mom if you date someone? Because that's stupid. Eddie's mom dates all the time, and she's a great mom. And you know Dad's introduced me to more girlfriends than I can count at this point—although I probably shouldn't have brought that up, since he's the furthest thing from a great father."

"Your father exposing you to a revolving door of random women is precisely why I didn't want to tell you about Grayson. Not until I'm sure he's going to be around for the long haul. You've already had enough random people coming in and out of your life. You don't need yet another random one, supplied by me."

"But Grayson isn't some 'random' guy at this point, obviously. After all this time, you and Grayson must care a lot about each other—unlike Dad and all of his gold diggers." He rolls his eyes. "I'd actually like to meet this guy to make sure he's good enough for you."

"Oh, he is. Grayson is so sweet. He treats me with total respect and kindness."

Drew narrows his eyes, like something I've said doesn't add up. "Then why keep him a secret for so long? Is there something about him you're still not sure about, like maybe you're making sure he's not after your money?"

"No, I'm positive Grayson cares about me for all the right reasons. He doesn't even know about my money. I mean, he knows I was married to your father, so I'm sure he supposes I'm fairly well off. But he's never even been to the house, and when I see him, I drive the Acura, instead of the Mercedes or the Porsche. I've never told him about Grandpa or even about my company. He thinks I *work* for a design company."

Drew furrows his brow. "Why haven't you told him the truth? If he can't handle Grandpa or knowing you're a badass businesswoman, then he's not the right guy for you, Mom. You always tell me not to change myself to make someone like me. So, follow your own advice."

"I don't change myself for Grayson. That's what makes my relationship with him so special. I'm totally myself with him, which I've been able to be since day one, since we've never had to talk about things that might be distracting or intimidating."

Drew isn't buying it. He flashes me a skeptical look I know all too well, since I frequently flash him the same one. "What aren't you telling me?" he asks. "Has he been to prison?"

I laugh. "No."

"Does he have a few baby mommas or something?"

"No, no. It's nothing like that." I take a deep breath. "The only tiny glitch is that Grayson is quite a bit younger than me."

Drew's eyebrows ride up. "How much younger?"

I twist my mouth. "He just turned twenty-six."

Drew's face lights up. "*Go, Mom*. Holy shit."

"Language, Drew," I say. But there's no authority in my tone. We both know that 'holy shit' was a perfect choice of words. When Drew rolls his eyes at my half-hearted chastisement, I add, "Grayson isn't the 'boy toy' you're probably envisioning. He's incredibly grounded and confident in his own skin. And he's smart, too. He created this amazing app that—"

"Mom, chill. Most of Dad's girlfriends are even younger than your dude. I'm not the one you have to convince. This is *your* hang-up, not mine."

I blush. "The thing is, I can't very well roll my eyes at your Peter Pan father, while doing exactly the same thing as him. And yet, that's exactly what I've been doing."

"Pfft. You're not doing the same thing as Dad. His girlfriends don't give a crap about him. Every single one of them thinks he's their meal ticket. I mean, if you don't *really* want to be with this guy, in your heart of hearts, that's fine. But if you're using his age or me as an excuse to—"

"No. I want to be with Grayson, without a doubt. He's the best, kindest, funniest, most loyal man I've ever known, and I couldn't find anyone better for me in ten lifetimes."

Drew raises his arms, his face clearly saying, "Then, what the fuck is the problem?"

I pause, gathering my thoughts. "I guess I figured things were going so well with him, why change anything that might rock the boat?"

Drew ponders that for a brief moment, before shrugging and saying, "It seems to me it wouldn't be the worst idea to rock the boat after a while to make sure it's as sturdy as you think it is." Again, he shrugs. "But what do I know? I'm fourteen."

I purse my lips and think, *"Out of the mouths of babes."*

Drew slides his hands into his jean pockets. "All I'm saying is you don't need to hide your boyfriend on my account." He winks and grins wickedly. "You're a smart woman, Mom. *I trust your judgment.*"

I narrow my eyes. Drew is echoing something I regularly say to him: "*You're a smart kid, Drew. I trust your judgment."*

"Thanks," I say.

Drew gestures toward the staircase. "Now, go on. Your 'naughty boy' is waiting for you with an extra-dirty vodka martini."

The little fucker. With my cheeks burning, I start walking toward the staircase, far too embarrassed to look my son in the eyes as I go.

"Is it okay if I sleep over at Eddie's tonight?" Drew calls to my back.

"Of course. Have fun."

"I guess that means if you want to finally have your boyfriend over, the house will be all yours."

"No, we've already made other plans, not that it's any of your business."

As I make my way down the staircase, I hear Drew calling Eddie from his room. Quickly, I gather my purse and overnight bag, since Grayson and I have booked a room at our usual hotel for the night. After shouting goodbye to Drew, I head outside, and two minutes later, I'm settling into the backseat of an Uber, since Grayson is planning to drive us from the restaurant to the hotel.

"That's a nice perfume," my female Uber driver says, as I latch my seatbelt.

"Thank you. My boyfriend gave it to me for Valentine's Day."

"What's it called? I'd like to get some."

"'True Love.'" I smile at the memory of Grayson giving me the purple perfume box, its name embossed in swirling gold script on its cover. Yet again, clever Grayson had found another way to tell me he loves me, without saying the actual words.

"Aw," the driver says. "That's sweet."

"My boyfriend is very sweet—the sweetest man I've ever met."

I look out the car window, as certainty washes over me. *He's so sweet*, I think, *I've just now decided I'm going to tell him I love him tonight, as soon as we walk into our hotel room. And once I've said the magic words and heard him say them back to me, I'm going to pounce on that sweet man and give him a night of hot sex he won't soon forget.*

12

GRAYSON

"To an amazing launch day!" Victoria says. She raises her glass, and everyone at our table—a group that includes Victoria, Selena and me, Victoria's business partner and his spouse, and the three amazing coders who've worked tirelessly alongside me for months—enthusiastically join the toast. A few more toasts are given, at which point another round of drinks are ordered and individual conversations begin blossoming around the table.

"On a personal note, Grayson," Victoria says. She leans in to be heard by only Selena and me at the table, as the rest of the group chatters enthusiastically among themselves. "Cheers to you for making my best friend the happiest I've ever seen her. That's saying a lot, given how long I've known her."

"No need to thank me," I say, shooting Selena a grin. "This woman makes me so damned happy; I keep pinching myself to see if I'm dreaming. But then I think, 'Stop pinching yourself, dummy! If this is a dream, don't wake yourself up!'"

Victoria and Selena giggle at my stupid joke and we slide into easy conversation about various, non-work-related things. After a bit, though, Selena places her linen napkin on the table and says, "Excuse me. I'm going to hit the ladies' room before the food arrives."

She winks at me as she rises, and then saunters away with her hips swinging, well aware I'm watching her gorgeous backside as she goes.

"So, Grayson," Victoria says, "I know we agreed not to talk too much shop tonight, but have you come to a decision about which industry we should micro-target next?"

"Yeah, actually. I've thought about it and . . ." I'm distracted when my phone on the table buzzes with a text from Selena. It reads, "Meet me in front of the restaurant. There's something urgent I need to tell you." Instantly, anxiety floods me. What urgent situation could possibly have arisen between Selena leaving for the bathroom and now? Did she leave the table because something was bothering her?

"And . . . what did you decide?" Victoria asks. "Don't leave me hanging, Gray."

"Sorry. I have to send a quick text. Forgive me."

With my heart lodged in my throat, I quickly tap out a reply text to Selena, asking her if everything is okay, and when she quickly replies that everything is wonderful, that I should meet her out front as soon as I can, I exhale with relief and rise from the table.

"Excuse me," I blurt. "I have to . . . say hello to an old friend I saw over there."

As I take my first few steps away, I try to walk slowly. Normally. Like my heart isn't crashing in my ears. But as soon as I've turned a corner and my dinner companions can't see me, I begin sprinting through the restaurant like a bat out of hell toward the front door. Selena's never summoned me like this before. What's going on?

Outside in the cold night, I'm relieved to find Selena looking anything but upset. In fact, she looks practically giddy—red-cheeked and bright-eyed, like a kid with a huge secret to spill.

"What's up?" I say, as I come to a stop before her.

Selena immediately takes both my hands. "Sorry if I worried you. I should have waited to talk to you at the hotel later. That was my plan. But all of a sudden, I couldn't wait another second to say this to you." She takes a deep breath. "Grayson McKnight, you're the best man I've ever known. You're a kind, brilliant, funny, loyal, sincere man, a true partner who makes me feel protected and loved like nobody else."

Holy fuck. Did Selena just use a form of the word *love*? She opens her mouth to continue, but I have to get this out first, before whatever words might be on the tip of her tongue. "I'm glad you feel loved," I choke out, as my heart clangs against my sternum. "Because I love you, Selena Diaz. With all my heart and soul."

Selena's face explodes with joy. "I love you, too! That's what I was about to say! I love you, Grayson McKnight! With all my heart and soul and with zero doubts or reservations!"

Elation floods me. I embrace her and clutch her to me. "I've wanted to tell you how much I love you for so long, and, hopefully, hear you say it back to me. This is a dream come true."

"Oh, honey," Selena says. "I'm so in love with you, I feel like a love-sick teenager, all the time. I feel physically high on my love for you."

With a beaming smile on my face, I lean in and kiss her, letting my lips and tongue put an exclamation point on the sacred words we've exchanged. When we finally disengage from our embrace, we're both practically levitating.

Selena bites her lower lip seductively. "Drew is spending the night at a friend's house tonight. Would you like to spend the night at my place, instead of the hotel?"

I whoop and fist-bump the cold air, making her laugh. But after we kiss again, I feel the need to make sure I haven't pressured her into this decision. "I only want you to take me home if you're sure," I insist. "If I've pressured you or—"

"No, not at all. I've waited way too long to bring you home. I'm excited."

"But why now? Only an hour ago on the phone, you said—"

"I know what I said. And I truly thought I meant it. But after we hung up, I discovered Drew eavesdropping on our call, and he set me straight."

A wave of panic washes over me. "Oh, fuck. Was I on speaker phone when Drew was listening?"

"Thank God, no. But even so, he heard enough of my end of the conversation—comments about you having a 'black, lace pair' and you being a 'naughty boy' for taking 'them'—to know our relationship is anything but platonic." She rolls her eyes. "It's all for the best, though, because my conversation with Drew made me realize I've been a damned fool. Way too careful. Not to mention, dishonest with you and myself."

"Dishonest? How so?"

Selena exhales. "The truth is I've been subconsciously using my son as an excuse not to let down all my walls with you. Not at first. I was right to be careful at first. But these days, I think I'm doing both of us a disservice by being so damned careful all the time." She shifts her weight. "I think the truth is I'm terrified to let down all my walls all the way, in case things don't work out for us in the end. I think I've convinced myself it'll hurt a whole lot less, if things go south on us, if I've kept a piece of me firmly guarded from heartbreak."

I touch her cheek. "Things are going to work out for us, my love. Of course, they are. And do you know how I know that? *Because you're my destiny.* Do you think it was random coincidence that woman at the bar gave me *your* number, of all the numbers in the entire world? Hell no. It was fate."

The look on Selena's face tells me she's deeply touched by my romanticism, even if she doesn't necessarily believe in fate the way I do. Either way, whether she believes in fate or not, when she throws her arms around my neck and kisses me passionately, I know Selena finally believes in *us*. She's finally all mine, and I'm all hers. No more doubts. No more fear. No more compartmentalization of her life to keep me separate from all the rest. From here on out, Selena is *finally* ready to throw caution to the wind and take our relationship to the next level, whatever form that takes.

We kiss and embrace, whispering words of love and adoration to each other as we do, even as people walk past on the busy sidewalk. Suddenly, though, Selena pulls back from our embrace and says, "We should probably head back inside, honey. We've been MIA from the dinner party for quite some time."

I grin wickedly. "*Or*—and hear me out on this—we could say you're not feeling well and ditch this popsicle stand right now, hightail it straight to your house, and fuck like amorous rabbits in every room of your house, all night long."

Selena giggles, but, unfortunately, she shakes her head. "Patience, my love. We have far too much to celebrate tonight, and too many people who rightfully want to revel in today's launch with you, to leave this party prematurely."

I exhale. She's right, of course.

"The silver lining," Selena adds, "is that anticipation can be a very sensual thing. It builds tension and excitement, which ultimately makes the sex even hotter."

"If you say so, Hot Teacher."

"Oh, I do, my little Grayson-hopper. You'll see."

With a sexy little smirk, she grabs my hand and pulls me toward the restaurant. But once we're inside, she stops walking long before we've reached our table, causing me to follow suit.

"Honey," she says with a crook of her finger. When I lean in, she adds, "Speaking of anticipation making things hotter . . . Throughout dinner, every time I squeeze your thigh underneath the table, it'll mean I'm thinking in that very moment, in graphic detail, about how much I can't wait to 'teabag' your balls when we get back to my house."

My mouth hangs open and my dick tingles. "Uh . . ."

Without waiting to hear whatever gibberish might come out of my mouth next, Selena saunters ahead of me toward our table, chuckling and swinging her hips, while I stagger behind her, the woman of my dreams, the love of my life, the last stop on my train, with a huge smile on my face, a massive boner in my pants, and my tongue practically dragging on the floor.

13
GRAYSON

"Turn left up here," Selena says, two seconds before the navigation app on my phone echoes the same instruction.

We're in my car, driving the route to Selena's address. And I can't help noticing we're headed toward an extremely affluent neighborhood, one with notably large, pricey homes overlooking Puget Sound. Does Selena live over here, or are we merely passing through?

I guess I should have pictured her living in a swanky neighborhood like this, seeing as how she was married to Andre De La Torre for twelve years. He's a flashy guy who obviously likes showing off his wealth. But Selena mentioned she'd bought her current house *after* her divorce, so I guess I let myself imagine her living in a normal, pretty house with her son and dog. I probably imagined her having a formal dining room, or a fancy living room she never uses, in addition to the usual living spaces—but certainly, I never pictured Selena living in a truly jaw-dropping house, the type that probably has a maid's quarters or guest house, like the enormous homes with perfect landscaping we're currently passing.

After a couple more turns, all the questions in my head are answered when Selena—and the navigation app—both direct me to turn into the driveway of a stunning two-story home. Selena's house isn't quite as large as some of the massive estates we've passed. But it's definitely not small. And with its location right on the water, not to mention the strikingly sprawling plot of land marked off by its perimeter fence, there's no way Selena's house wouldn't command a multi-million-dollar price tag.

"This is pretty," I murmur as I park my car in the circular driveway. It's an understatement. A bit of deadpan humor. By any measure, this house is stunning. The kind I've never imagined I'd get to enter in my lifetime, let alone sleep overnight in, especially at the invitation of the great love of my life.

"Thank you," Selena says in earnest, apparently not understanding my attempt at understated humor. "It's my dream home."

"I can see why." I turn to look at Selena in my passenger seat, and the warm smile on her face chases away my nerves. Who cares where she lives, or how big her bank balance might be? No matter what, Selena is still the same loving, grounded, kind-hearted woman I'm head over heels in love with. Nothing, literally nothing, not even the fact that she lives in a mini-mansion I could never afford to give her in a hundred lifetimes could possibly change that.

"The bad news," I say, "is that I don't think we're going to be able to pull off fucking like amorous rabbits in every room of your house in one night, like I suggested at the restaurant, no matter how hard we try. That job is going to take at least a full week. Maybe more."

Selena winks. "It'll be fun trying, though." She touches my forearm. "Is there good news, though?"

"Yeah, I was going to say the good news is that it'll be fun trying, but you stole my thunder."

She chuckles. "Sorry."

"That's okay. I've got a back-up plan. The *new* good news is that we've got all the time in the world."

Selena's dark eyes sparkle. "We sure do, my love."

I take a deep breath and speak on my exhale. "Stay put, goddess. I'll get your door for you."

"Such a gentleman."

My heart thundering with excitement, I jog around the back of my car and open the passenger door, and Selena leads me toward her porch. As we walk, she tells me about some flower boxes along the walkway she planted last weekend.

"And after all that hard work, Daisy promptly destroyed half of them," she says. "Fucking dog."

I laugh. "I can't wait to see Daisy on her home turf."

By now, I've interacted with Selena's beloved pooch lots of times during hikes and at various dog parks. But the idea of me getting to hang out with Selena and her dog like normal couples do—while watching a movie or having a barbeque in her backyard—her extremely large backyard, as it turns out—is for some reason ridiculously thrilling to me.

"I'm sure Daisy will be ecstatic to show you each and every one of her toys," Selena says. "I'm guessing she'll go to her toy box and pull each one out to bring to you."

"I can't wait."

We reach the porch and stop in front of the door. "Okay, when we first walk in, ignore Daisy completely if she jumps on you. I'm sure she'll go apeshit when she sees you, and if you ignore her until she's a good girl, she'll calm down quicker."

"Got it."

We enter the foyer of the house, and precisely as warned, Selena's huge dog excitedly tackles me, rising onto her back legs to give me an almost-human hug.

"Down, Daisy," Selena says.

"Hi, baby," I say, embracing and petting Daisy enthusiastically. "It's great to see you, too, baby."

"Ignore her, Grayson."

"Sorry. I forgot."

I drop my arms to my sides, while Selena chastises the dog and commands her to sit. Finally, Daisy plants her ass onto the hardwood floor at my feet, like the bestest girl she is—although she's wagging her tail so damned hard, I'm worried it's going to detach from her quaking body and hurtle against a wall any second now—and Selena tells me I'm now permitted to give the trembling dog affection as her reward for obedience.

After we give Daisy lots of scratches and pets in the foyer, Selena leads me into the next room—a formal living room that's straight out of a magazine.

"Whoa, Selena, this is beautiful."

"Thank you."

"You decorated it yourself?"

"Absolutely. Everything you see is exactly the way I wanted it."

"I can tell. It's so *you*."

She's beaming. "Would you like a cocktail for the full tour?"

"I'd love one."

Selena waggles her eyebrows. "Or maybe we could skip the full tour for now and take our cocktails out back to the hot tub?"

"Sounds great."

She squeals. "I'm so happy you're here." With a little shimmy, Selena takes my hand and leads me through the living room and into the next—a family room, apparently—which I presume is the route toward the kitchen. But when we enter the expansive room, we're surprised to discover we're not alone in the house. Four teenagers—two boys and two girls—are spread out on a large, L-shaped leather couch.

When we appear in the entryway to the room, one of the boys—I'm surmising he's Drew—leaps up, his mouth the shape of an "O," and shouts "Mom! What are you doing home?"

"Drew!" Selena says. "What are *you* doing home? You're supposed to be at Eddie's!"

"Hi, Mrs. De La Torre," the other boy says, as he leaps up to standing alongside Drew.

"Hello, Eddie," Selena says, her voice tinged with skepticism. "Drew told me he'd be staying the night at your house tonight."

The boys look at each other, both faces telegraphing they've been caught in a lie.

"There was a change of plans at the last minute," Drew says quickly, his face the color of a beet. "You said you'd be gone all night, so we figured we'd watch a movie here."

"Yes, with these two lovely girls, I see," Selena fires back, her tone making it clear Drew's ass is firmly in a sling.

The two girls have been fidgeting awkwardly on the couch throughout the entire exchange, but at Selena's mention of them, they both grimace like they've stuck their fingers into a light socket. I catch the wide gaze of one of them and flash her a reassuring smile, letting her know she's perfectly safe here, not in trouble in any way, and she returns my smile before looking down at her painted toenails.

"I don't mind you having friends over, Drew," Selena continues. She adds pointedly, "*When you've cleared it with me.*" She looks at the girls, and her tone shifts to something a bit less stern. "Don't worry, girls. You've done nothing wrong but accept an invitation my son *knew* he wasn't authorized to extend." She returns to her son. "Drew, you know full-well you can't have friends over when I don't know about it, and you especially can't have a party here after you've *lied* to me about where you'd be."

"It wasn't a lie when I said it," Drew insists. "Our plans just kind of . . . changed. And this isn't a party, Mom. Nobody else is coming. It's just the four of us—and we're doing nothing but watching a movie."

I press my lips together, trying not to laugh at the kid's

obvious discomfort. Clearly, we've barged in on a double date. One that looks pretty innocent, if you ask me, considering how far apart the kids were sitting when we first walked in on them.

Selena doesn't seem to share my amusement. With her nostrils flaring, she addresses the two girls again. "Do your parents know where you are, ladies?"

"Yes, ma'am," the girl with the painted toenails says. "My curfew is eleven on weekends. They track my phone, so they know where I am."

"And I'm spending the night at her house," the other girl squeaks out, looking like she wants to barf. "My parents don't track my phone, though, I don't think. Please, don't tell them about this."

Selena glances at me and whatever levity she sees in my eyes causes her to narrow hers and flash me a warning look that practically screams, *Don't you dare laugh.*

"My mom is coming at quarter to eleven to pick everyone up," Eddie interjects. "She knows we're here. She's going to drop the girls off and then bring Drew and me back to my house."

"Eddie, tell me the truth," Selena says. "Your mother thinks I've been here with you this whole time, correct?"

Eddie drops his head. "Yes, ma'am."

Again, Selena looks at me and it's all I can do not to grin at her. Was there any doubt that's what the kids told Eddie's mom—and, surely, Painted Toenail Girl's parents, as well—that Selena would be here to chaperone the kids throughout the entire movie? Selena has mentioned Drew attends a private Catholic school. If all of these kids are schoolmates of Drew's, as I suspect, then it's likely they're all being raised in fairly strict homes, at least by my standards. Which means every kid in this room is currently shitting a brick.

"We're still sleeping at Eddie's tonight," Drew assures his mother. "Eddie and I only came here to watch a horror movie, since our screen is way bigger, and I'd offered to be the one to pay the rental fee, which I'll do out of my allowance." He motions toward the screen, where a maniacal clown is currently frozen on pause. "And while we were walking over here, Eddie and I got the idea to ask Sophia and Carina if they wanted to come over and watch the movie with us, since they said at lunch the other day they were dying to see this one, and we figured, 'Why let them spend the money to rent it, when we're already renting it ourselves?'."

Somehow, Selena's managed to wear a poker face throughout the entirety of her son's panicked ramblings. Without a hint of amusement, she replies evenly, "How thoughtful of you, Drew."

"Exactly! You've taught me to be thoughtful, whenever I can, so that's all I was trying to do, Mom."

I have to bite my tongue not to let out a loud chortle. *Sure it was, buddy. You and Eddie were only saving these two pretty girls a movie rental fee.*

Selena's eyes meet mine, ever so briefly, before she returns to Drew and says, "All right. You can go ahead and watch the movie. Next time, however, if your plans change and you're not where you said you'd be, text me your location. Also, ask my permission before inviting friends over. You know the rules."

I can tell Drew wants to roll his eyes something fierce, but, somehow, the boy manages to nod obediently and say, "I will." One side of his mouth hitches up, ever so slightly. "Speaking of changed plans, are you going to introduce me to your unexpected guest, Mother?"

That chortle I suppressed earlier? Yeah, it hurtles out of me, against my will. Luckily, I quickly manage to contain myself when Selena glares at me, telling me to get myself under control. But there's zero doubt Drew heard it and therefore knows I find this entire situation highly amusing.

Selena clears her throat and gestures primly to me. "Drew,

this is my friend, Grayson McKnight. Grayson, this is my son, Drew, and his best friend since pre-school, Eddie, and their two lovely friends whom I've never met before tonight."

Drew supplies the girls' names, before asking his mother, "So, Grayson here is your *friend*?"

"That's right," Selena replies, her face a deep shade of crimson.

I walk toward Drew, my hand extended. "Hello, Drew."

The kid meets me halfway and shakes my hand firmly. And for the life of me, when my eyes lock with his, I can't resist shooting the kid a smirk that lets him know I find the "friend" label laughable, too.

While shaking my hand, the kid says, "Hello, Grayson—my mother's *friend*."

"I'm thrilled to finally meet you," I say, releasing him. "I've heard great things about you."

Drew slides his hands into his pockets and flashes his mother a snide look, even as he replies to me. "Oh yeah? That's weird. Because my mother has said absolutely nothing about you, Grayson. Not until earlier tonight, that is." He returns to me and smiles warmly. "At which point, I heard nothing but great things about you, too."

We share an easy, amused grin of understanding that makes me feel certain I'm going to like this kid.

"Glad to hear it," I say.

Selena clears her throat. "We'll let you kids get back to watching the movie now, so you can be sure to finish before Eddie's mom arrives."

"And we'll let you get back to hanging out with your *friend*," Drew says, his mouth lopsided with amusement. "Oh, hey, do we have any popcorn, Mom? I looked but couldn't find any."

"You must not have looked too hard. I bought some last week."

Drew flashes his mother a charming smile. "Would you make some for us, Mother Dear? *Please*?"

Selena chuckles. "You don't need to pour it on quite that thick, sweetie. I'd love some popcorn, too. Come on, Grayson. I'll show you the kitchen."

"Bye, everyone," I say with a clipped wave to the group, before shooting one last smile at Drew, which he, thankfully, returns with ease. In fact, if I'm not mistaken, the smile that kid is shooting me is saying, *It's about fucking time.*

14
GRAYSON

"That went so well!" I whisper excitedly, following Selena out of the family room. "Drew actually smiled at me, and it didn't look forced at all."

Selena doesn't speak. It's only when we reach the kitchen that she finally says something, but it's not in reply to my comment. "That little Casanova!" she huffs out. "He only wanted to save those girls a rental fee, did he? Ha!"

While Selena marches defiantly into the heart of her kitchen, I stop short in the doorway, too stunned by the gorgeousness sprawling before me to speak. Selena's kitchen is enormous and gleaming—the kind featured on gourmet cooking shows and in movies about insanely wealthy people.

"Holy shit, Selena," I murmur. "Your kitchen is right out of a movie."

She puts her hands on her hips and spits out, "Drew thought he'd have the Playboy Mansion all to himself for his little party, did he?" She's practically breathing fire. "The little fucker!"

I can't help chuckling at her word choice. "For what it's worth, Drew's 'party' looked pretty damned innocent to me."

"*Innocent?*" Selena scoffs. "My son *intentionally* lied to me—straight to my face. He said he'd be staying at Eddie's tonight."

"And he will be, right after his hot date."

Selena shoots me daggers. "He lied and broke the rules."

I shrug. "Yeah, so he and his buddy could watch a movie with a couple of pretty girls. I think that's pretty standard stuff."

Selena narrows her eyes. "My son can break whatever rules he wants, when he's an adult. But he'll follow my rules when he's living under my roof."

I try with all my might to bite back a smile, but it's easier said than done. This 'angry MILF' side of Selena is new to me—and I've gotta say, it's sexy as hell. In fact, the sight of her looking so fucking pissed about Drew's supposedly unthinkable behavior is sending rockets of desire shooting through my bloodstream and straight to my dick.

"Fair enough," I say before pressing my lips together in a way that says, "I'll shut the fuck up now."

Selena scrutinizes my features for a long beat. And then, "Okay, out with it." She crosses her arms. "Tell me whatever it is you're thinking."

"I'm not a parent. I'm sure I've already said too much."

"Well, don't stop now. Tell me what you're thinking." She beckons. "Go on."

I shrug. "I'm mostly thinking you're scorching-hot when you're infuriated. Damn, Selena. I didn't know there was another level to your hotness. Whew!"

She blushes.

"I'm also thinking Drew isn't quite the juvenile delinquent you're making him out to be. If I'd had enough confidence as a teenager to speak to a pretty girl at all, let alone to invite her to my house to watch a movie, I sure as hell would have done it, even if it meant breaking one of my mother's rules. And I'm sure I'd feel particularly justified in my lawlessness if, earlier that day, I'd discovered my mother had been hiding a boyfriend from me—aka 'lying to me about him'—for the past six months." I wait for her reply. And when it doesn't come, I add, "But, mostly, I was thinking you're hot as fuck when you're spitting fire."

Selena leans her hip against the kitchen island and flashes me a begrudging smile. "You think I'm hot—even in this context?"

"You mean, in the context of you being a mom?"

She nods.

"Are you kidding me?" I blurt. "What's the only thing hotter than a MILF? *An enraged MILF.*" When she laughs, I walk to her and place my palms on her hips. "Watching you read Drew the Riot Act made me want to drag you upstairs to your bedroom and fuck you till you're screaming my name."

Selena blushes and whispers, "*Grayson.*"

"Yeah, just like that. Only much louder."

She chuckles. "If I look enraged, it's because I am. I hate lying in any form, and Drew knows it."

"I'm sure he fully respects that, especially after everything you went through with his father. Drew knows about that, right?"

She nods. "The gist."

"But the thing is," I say, "do you really want your teenage son to tell you about every last thought in his head? At a certain point, once the hormones start kicking in, I think some things are better left unsaid between a mom and her son. I certainly didn't tell my mother every damned thing I thought or did during my teenage years, but that didn't mean I loved or respected her any less."

Selena grimaces. "You keep using the word *teenager.*"

"Right. Because that's what Drew is. Hence, the word four*teen.*"

"He only turned fourteen last month."

"And before then, he was thir-*teen*." I laugh at her scowl. "There's no way around it, Mama. Your kid's a teenager. Sorry to inform you."

"Ugh." She leans into me and puts her forehead on my shoulder. "I'm *so* not ready for this."

I stroke her back. "If it makes you feel any better, the kids were sitting so far apart when we first walked in on them, I'm positive you've got at least a couple years before Drew's hosting secret orgies at your house."

Selena gasps. "Grayson McKnight!" She swats my shoulder. "Don't say that word in relation to my sweet little baby boy!"

I laugh. "I was trying to comfort you."

"By saying my son will soon be having secret orgies in my house?"

"Chin up. He might decide to co-host them at Eddie's house, instead."

"Stop teasing me. You're giving me a heart attack." She leans her luscious ass against the island, exhales, and tilts her head back. "All joking aside, I'm terrified Drew will turn out like his father—addicted to sex and an expert at lying about it. My main goal in life is to make sure I'm not raising a clone of Andre."

"Sweetheart, Drew won't turn out anything like his asshole father," I assure her. I touch a lock of her dark hair. "And do you know how I know? Because he's got *you* as his mother. Thanks to you and your incredible parenting, Drew will learn to respect every single woman he . . . invites-to-secret-orgies-whenever-his-mother-goes-out-for-the-night."

"Grayson!"

I burst out laughing, and, luckily, Selena joins me.

"You're incorrigible," she says. "Please, no more talk about my son's future orgies. My poor heart truly can't take it."

"That was the last time. I swear on my love for you."

"Thank you." She thinks for a moment before unleashing an amused smirk. "Did you see the boys' faces when they first saw us? They looked like all the oxygen had suddenly been sucked out of their bodies."

I laugh. "We were definitely a buzzkill, dude."

Selena snickers. "Do you think the kids were hoping to do something more salacious tonight than watch a movie, but we foiled their big plans?"

I pretend to consider the question, even though the answer is obvious. "Well, I have no idea what the girls were thinking. But based on my experience as a fourteen-year-old boy, I can confidently say that *yes,* the boys were fervently hoping and praying something more salacious than watching a movie would transpire tonight."

Selena laughs and slides her arms around my torso. "I'm so glad you're here to talk me off the proverbial ledge."

"I'm at your service, ma'am. In fact, I'll give you a promo code, so you can use my talking-off-the-ledge services any time, day or night, free of charge."

"What a deal."

I kiss her. "Thank you for letting me see your home. Are you upset I unexpectedly got to meet Drew, so much earlier than you'd planned?"

"No. Left to my own devices, I would have waited far too long. Now that you're here, it feels like perfect timing."

My heart leaps. "I'm so glad you feel that way."

Selena's chest heaves. "In fact, now that you've met Drew and he obviously likes you, I think you should join us for dinner or a movie night sometimes. Maybe once a week? And you can stay the night whenever Drew is sleeping at Andre's or a friend's house."

"Awesome."

"Beyond that, I think we should keep seeing each other away from my house, as we've been doing. I want to integrate you into Drew's home life slowly, okay? I don't want to give him, or myself, whiplash."

"Your house, your rules, baby. We'll do this on your timeline."

Selena sighs with relief. "Thank you. I really appreciate that." She pauses. "There's something I should tell you, Grayson. Something I probably should have mentioned a long time ago."

I wait with my heart thrumming.

Selena pauses. And then, "I don't work at a design company. I *own* the company where I work."

My shoulders soften. *That's it?* I can't fathom why she felt the need to keep this from me all this time, since it only accentuates what a brilliant, high-achieving, kick-ass woman she is. Did she think this information would negatively affect my opinion of her? The very notion is preposterous. I say, "That doesn't surprise me at all. I already knew you're a badass. Do you have any employees, or are you a one-woman show?"

"I have over thirty employees spread out over two offices in Seattle and Portland. We provide design services throughout the Pacific Northwest."

"You're a mogul!"

Selena laughs. She's lit up like a Christmas tree. "I started my company on a wing and a prayer after my divorce. And to my surprise, within six months, I had more clients and jobs than I could handle on my own. I had to keep hiring people to service all the work pouring in."

"Why were you surprised? You're always going to succeed at whatever you try, Selena. That's who you are."

She looks sheepish. "In the beginning, I think a lot of jobs came from powerful people who'd found out I was divorcing Andre De La Torre. He's got a lot of enemies in this town. That's been good for business."

"Even so," I say, "that's not why people *continued* to hire you, and refer you, and love your work."

Selena's chest visibly swells. "I'm proud to say the vast majority of jobs these days come from repeat clients and referrals."

"See? I know what I'm talking about. What kinds of design services does your company provide?"

"Interior design for luxury commercial brands and properties. Our bread-and-butter is staging luxury model homes, but we also do a lot of work for hotels, offices, restaurants, VIP boxes at stadiums, nightclubs."

"No wonder your house looks like a model home. You're a pro. Will you take me to see some of the model homes you've worked on? And anything else you've done, too. I want to see it all."

Selena's practically glowing with excitement. "I'd be thrilled to show you. Thank you for wanting to see my work."

"I want to know everything there is to know about you, Selena."

She blushes. "I want to know everything about you, too."

I laugh. "You already do. That's the difference between you and me."

She doesn't deny it.

"What made you decide to start your own design company?"

"It was thanks to my father. After the divorce, I was at my lowest, not knowing quite what to do with myself, if I wasn't Mrs. Andre De La Torre. I was thinking about applying for a job as an interior designer, but my father said, 'Nah, don't work for someone else. Start your own thing.' He offered me money to get started, which I wouldn't accept. I told him I wanted to build my company on my own, the same way he'd done with his first business. But I did accept his encouragement and invaluable business advice."

"Your father owns a business?"

She nods. "Several. He started out owning a single home goods store when he first came to America. That one store ultimately became two, and then ten, and then twenty, until a huge national chain bought him out." Selena names the chain—a household name—and I suddenly realize what she's actually telling me. *She's loaded.* Or at least, her father is. She continues, "After the sale, my father invested the proceeds in real estate and several businesses, and it was like he's got a Midas Touch."

I now understand why Selena didn't tell me any of this before now. She wanted to be sure I'd like her for *her*. I can't fathom Selena ever thinking I'm some kind of money-grubber or sweetheart swindler. So, that's not it. But she clearly wanted to give me the chance to get to know her without the risk of me feeling insecure about my humble lifestyle and upbringing compared to hers. "I'd love to meet your father," I blurt, and then instantly wish I could stuff the words back into my mouth.

It took Selena six months to invite me to her house, after all. And if Drew hadn't unexpectedly been here tonight, she wouldn't have introduced me to him until our one-year anniversary. How could I possibly think she'd be willing to introduce me, her twenty-six-year-old boyfriend with a small start-up, to her beloved mogul of a father? She's told me their bond has always been especially tight, ever since the death of Selena's mother when she was small. And that her father was always a strict, protective father, so much so that he didn't let her date till she was eighteen. Enter Andre. So how could I possibly think Selena would even consider introducing me to her father on a timeline any shorter than the one she was planning for my introduction to her kid?

"My father wants to meet you, too," Selena says, much to my shock. "I told him about you during my Uber ride to the restaurant this evening, and he told me to set something up."

My heart leaps. "Any time."

Selena flashes me a breathtaking smile. "Thank you for

wanting to meet my family and for taking all of this new information in stride."

"I love you, Selena. Nothing will change that. Not the fact that you're a badass businesswoman. Not your big house."

"Not even my smartass kid?"

I laugh. "Drew is awesome."

It's all true, of course. But I can't deny, throughout this entire exchange, an unbidden thought keeps entering my mind. Namely, *Why the hell has Selena picked me, out of all the men in the world, when she could have literally anyone?*

"Uh oh," Selena says, narrowing her dark eyes. "What's wrong?"

"Nothing. Today is the best day of my life."

Selena isn't buying it. "Tell me what you're thinking, Grayson."

"That I love you. That I'm the luckiest guy in the world."

She cocks her head. "No, it's something else. You just now had a thought that made you anxious, and now you're clearly choosing not to tell me about it—and that makes me nervous."

Goddamn, my fucking face. "It's nothing. For a split-second there, I couldn't help thinking, basically, 'What could I possibly give her that she doesn't already have?' But I'm not having some big, existential crisis about it. It was a fleeting thought."

Selena touches my cheek. "What could you possibly give me? That's an easy one, Grayson. *Your heart. Your love.* Honey, don't you know you love me like nobody ever has? You love me like I've only ever dreamed of being loved."

I blush. "Thank you. I love you with everything I am."

"I know that. I can feel it. And that's how I love you back. That's everything to me." She smiles. "Now, kiss me, you silly, gorgeous fool of a man, and never let me catch you wondering what's in it for me to love you, ever again."

"Yes, ma'am. *MILF.*" I lean in to kiss her but jerk back abruptly at the sound of Drew's voice in the doorway.

"Mom?" he says. "What happened to the popcorn?"

"Oh, shit," Selena says. She turns toward her son, flustered. "Sorry, I got distracted."

The kid comes to a stop at the far end of the island. "There's only twenty minutes left in the movie. We paused to take a quick bathroom break."

"I'll make it right now."

She scurries off to get popping, while Drew rests his forearms on the island and looks at me. "Hey, do you play Dungeons & Dragons, by any chance?"

"I'm a computer nerd," I say. "Of course, I do." It's a half-truth. I played once in middle school and sucked so badly, I got disinvited to play again. But he's obviously asking for a reason, and there's no way in hell I'm missing out on any opportunity to find common ground with Selena's son.

"Would you be willing to fill in for a player this week?" Drew asks. "He got grounded and isn't allowed to play, and all of the encounters in my campaign—I'm the DM—were balanced for six players."

I have no idea what the fuck he's talking about. But what I say is, "Oof. That sounds like a tough spot."

Drew nods. "No self-respecting DM would let there be a TPK, right?"

"Hell no," I say. "Not on your watch." I'm pretty sure "DM" means "Dungeon Master" or "Dragon Master." Meaning Drew is the one in charge of the game. But I make a mental note to google "TPK." Also, the general rules of play, since standing here now I can't remember any of them.

"So, you'll play? It'd only be a one-time thing."

"Yeah, I could probably help you out, depending on when and where."

"We play online over voice chat, so you could play anywhere. But since Eddie usually comes over here to play, it'd be cool if you came here, too."

"Great. When?"

"Thursday at seven."

Selena interjects, "Shoot. Thursday is the only night Grandpa can do dinner this week. You'll have to reschedule the game."

"We can't. Thursday is the only night everyone is free, Mom," Drew says. "Can't we start the game later than usual and play after dinner? Grandpa always leaves around eight-thirty."

"Okay, as long as you don't play past eleven."

"Eleven-thirty?"

Selena pauses and narrows her eyes, but I'm guessing she's only doing it for dramatic effect. "All right. Just this once."

"Thanks, Mom." Drew looks at me. "You should come to dinner before the game." He looks at his mother with a mischievous smile on his face. "Unless you're planning to keep Grayson a secret from grandpa a while longer?"

With a roll of her eyes, Selena walks toward us with a huge bowl of popcorn in her hands. "As a matter of fact, I was planning to invite Grayson to this week's family dinner. I just wanted to make sure you'd be comfortable with it first."

Drew pulls a face like Selena's comment is ridiculous. "I'm the one who told you to stop hiding your secret boyfriend in the first place, remember? The real question is if you're comfortable introducing him to Grandpa. Although, in my opinion, you shouldn't care what Grandpa thinks of Grayson. Who cares that he'll see that your secret boyfriend can't grow a beard to save his life. Who cares if Grandpa finds out Grayson not only knows how to play Dungeons & Dragons, but he's also geeked out of his mind to play with a bunch of fourteen-year-olds? All that matters is that you like him, exactly the way he is, and he treats you right."

A chortle escapes my mouth. *Damn. The kid's a fucking savage.*

"*Andrew De La Torre,*" Selena chastises. "You're being rude. Apologize to Grayson."

"That's not necessary," I interject. I flash Drew a big, goofy smile that nonverbally confirms he's pegged me right, top to bottom—especially the part about me being totally geeked to spend time with him—and Drew returns my smile with one of his own. I add, "There wasn't a false word spoken."

With a scolding glare, Selena hands her son the bowl of popcorn. "Go on," she says. "Get back to your party. You know, the one you brazenly lied to my face about?"

Drew tosses a popped kernel into his mouth. "Off I go, Mother Dear. Thanks for the popcorn. Have fun, kids." As he saunters away, he tosses over his shoulder, "I'm looking forward to Thursday, Grayson."

"Me, too."

"Really?" he replies, his tone playful. "I couldn't tell."

"*Drew*," Selena chastises. But I can't help smiling. Yup. He's definitely got me pegged. I'm the human equivalent of a Golden Retriever, and I can't even pretend otherwise.

When Drew is gone, I exhale and say, "And here I thought he'd invited me to play his little reindeer game because he likes me. But it was only to make fun of my shiny, red nose."

Selena makes a sympathetic face. "He does like you. He gave you a hard time as a means of indirectly razzing *me* for hiding you for so long. He does like you, though. It's obvious."

"I like him, too. The kid is whip smart."

"More like a smartass."

I slide my palms across her hips and rest them on her ample ass. "I know how much you value honesty, so I feel like I should confess: I lied to your son just now. I don't actually remember how to play Dungeons & Dragons. I played it once in middle school and sucked so badly, they never invited me back."

Selena laughs. "That's what Google is for." She lays her cheek against my chest and squeezes me tight. "I can't believe how good it feels to have you here. How natural it feels for you to meet Drew. I thought it would be this big, scary thing, but it felt so right."

I kiss the top of her head. "That's because we're meant to be, baby. We're fate—and nothing and nobody will ever convince me otherwise."

15
SELENA

"Don't let the door hit ya on the way out, kids!" I sing out through my toothy smile, which causes Grayson to chuckle next to me. We're standing shoulder-to-shoulder on my front porch, waving pleasantly to the four teenagers climbing into Eddie's mom's SUV. And not a moment too soon, I might add.

"Bye now, ya little cock-blockers," Grayson adds, through his wide smile. Which, in turn, makes me laugh even harder.

The minute the SUV disappears around a corner, I shout, "Freedom!" before grabbing Grayson's hand and practically dragging him toward my front door. "It's finally time for you to fuck me in my own bed, baby."

"Yes, MILF."

We enter the foyer. "Is this going to be a *thing*?" I ask playfully. "You calling me 'MILF?'"

Grayson shrugs. "Only when I'm turned on. As a horny teenager, fucking a hot MILF in her big, fancy house was one of my hottest fantasies."

"How fun for me to be able to make your teenage fantasies a reality."

Midway up the staircase, when Grayson asks a question about one of the many family photos on the wall, I pause on a step and pivot toward him.

"Sweetheart, I promise I'll tell you every story behind every photo—*after* you've fucked me into complete exhaustion in my bed. But right now, I want your eyeballs staring at my ass in your face as we climb the staircase and your brain focused on what you're going to do to make me come."

Grayson smiles. "Yes, MILF." He pinches my ass when I continue climbing the staircase and murmurs, "That's one hell of a bitable ass."

In my bedroom, we lose our clothes with record speed and crash into each other with hungry lips. For a few moments, we kiss and grope each other's naked flesh in the middle of my bedroom, letting our arousal rise and heat to a near-boil, at which point we move to the bed and begin making out horizontally.

"I can't believe I'm finally here with you," Grayson gasps out, as his steely hard-on nudges into my bare thigh

I stroke his erection. "Having you here is a dream come true."

"*You're* a dream come true." With that, he crawls between my legs and proceeds to eat and finger me exuberantly, eventually pulling a rippling orgasm out of me that makes me shudder and growl as it warps my core, and then mew like a kitten as it rolls through my extremities.

When my climax subsides, I crook my finger suggestively, prompting Grayson to scale the length of my torso like a horny rock-climber. As his face approaches mine, I'm turned on by the sight of him. His lips and chin are shiny from his meal. His arm muscles are taut, and his newly acquired six-pack noticeably cut.

When his face reaches mine, Grayson places his forearms on either side of my head, exhales a shaky breath, and nudges his beefy tip against my wet entrance. I moan with anticipation, but when it's clear that's as far as he's going for now, I grip his ass with greedy palms and nonverbally instruct him to push inside and fill me up. I'm salivating with lust by now. Physically quaking with the need to be filled to the brink by this man's thick cock. But even more so, to fuse my body with his, my soul with his—to tell him I love him while he's fucking my brains out.

Grayson kisses me deeply, while continuing to tease me with his slick tip lodged at my entrance. After a bit, he slides his tip urgently against my clit, and the effect is like I've gripped an electric fence.

"Oh, God, get inside me," I gasp out, breaking free from his kiss. I'm panting. Clutching his ass and physically pushing him inside me.

Grayson's breathing is ragged. His smile is wicked. As he continues rubbing his tip against me, he says, "You're the one who said anticipation can be a good thing, remember? And then proceeded to turn me on all through dinner. So, you can wait."

I suddenly remember the implied promise I made to Grayson throughout dinner, with each squeeze of his thigh underneath the table. How could I forget about that until now?

"Bring your cock to my mouth," I whisper. "There's something I've been dying to do to you all night."

As his entire body trembles with excitement, Grayson rearranges himself to get into position to fuck my face. "Not to completion, baby," he whispers. "I'm not leaving this room without fucking you in your bed."

"No argument from me."

He grips my headboard, places his knees on either side of my face, and offers his beefy tip to my lips. Without hesitation, I begin licking and lapping at his tip and shaft, before taking his balls into my mouth. I suck each testicle enthusiastically until he's groaning in a way that would make me smile if my mouth weren't otherwise engaged. When his noises become desperate, I release his balls and lick his cock again, and finally take his entire length into my mouth and down my throat with energetic zeal.

Grayson makes a guttural sound that only gets louder and more desperate as my energetic blowjob continues. *And I love it.* It's funny. During my marriage, I gave my husband head all the fucking time. Frankly, it was a part-time job. An exhausting one which, I later realized, was a manifestation of the power dynamic in our relationship. I gave to my husband, and he took and took but never gave. I thought that was normal, because he was my only lover, my teacher—the one with the expertise—and he obviously assumed that was the natural order of things.

But with Grayson, everything is different. Giving this sweet man a blowjob makes me feel powerful. Sexy. Turned on. I *love* pushing Grayson to the brink of pure ecstasy with my mouth. I love knowing I've got the power to make him feel like he's physically overdosing on pure bliss, any ol' time I please.

Speaking of which, all signs point to Grayson being on the cusp of an overdose right now. As he grunts and quakes, I grope his balls and taint enthusiastically, while my mouth continues its hungry work. And, finally, I slide my fingertip to his anus and press down, causing his entire body to jolt.

"Oh, God," Grayson grits out. Without warning, he abruptly pulls out of my mouth and murmurs, "Close call." He scrambles into position on top of me, whispering, "You're one talented MILF." And two seconds later, he's on top of me, kissing me passionately.

I open my legs wide while gripping his naked ass, and he slides a finger inside me, apparently zeroing in on his target, before finally, blessedly, sinking himself inside me.

As Grayson's girth and length stretches and fills me to the brink, I moan loudly along with him. And when he begins thrusting enthusiastically, I wrap my thighs around his hips, move my pelvis with his, and tell him I love him. I'm not merely having sex with Grayson's body—I'm making love to his very soul. I feel a palpable cord of energy, love, and light connecting our bodies as we move together. I feel safe. Seen. Loved. Whatever contradictions are tangled up inside me, they all somehow make perfect sense when I'm with this man. He accepts and loves all of me, and I'm finally ready to let him love every part of me, no matter how imperfect any particular part might be.

"I love you so much," Grayson whispers, right before he jerks and comes with a long, deep groan.

When his body quiets down, he fingers me, briefly, making me come again. And finally, we lie next to each other in the bed, sweaty and satisfied.

He takes my hand. "I love you," he whispers.

"I love you, too," I whisper back.

Forever.

That's the word that pops into my mind.

But I don't say it out loud. For now, it's enough to tell him I love him. For now, that's as big a step as I'm willing to take. As much as I love Grayson, I'm still well aware we're at different stages of our lives. At this point, I'm not a woman who believes in fairytales that end in happily ever after, no matter how sweet and sincere the applicant for the job of Prince Charming.

16

SELENA

"Oh, God, *yes!*" I shriek at the top of my lungs. "Stay hard for me! Hang on!"

For our second round of this first night together in my house, Grayson and I are having frenzied, drunken sex in my hot tub. I'm riding on top of him this time, gripping his wet hair as I do like it's a flotation device and I'm a tipsy vacationer who fell overboard in stormy seas. Grayson, for his part, is clutching my hips underneath the warm water with a sexy ferocity that equals my grip on his hair.

In terms of stamina, it's a lucky thing Grayson came an hour ago in my bed and has now had quite a bit to drink. But even so, it's plain to see the poor man is now valiantly holding on for dear life underneath me.

"Don't come yet," I bark. "And don't change the angle of your cock! It's in the exact, perfect spot for me to . . ." My most intimate muscles begin warping and rippling. "Ooooooh, *God. Yesss.*" I quickly lift myself off Grayson's cock and shove my tits into his face. If I let him experience my orgasm with his cock buried inside me, he'll come, too. Without a doubt. And I'm not ready to give up my human dildo yet. I'm still way too horny for that.

Without hesitation, Grayson begins motorboating my breasts, so I fist his wet hair and smash his face into my wet skin as he devours me. Soon, I'm so turned on, I yank his head back and say something I've never said to anyone else in my life: "Babe, I want you to fuck me up the ass."

Grayson's green eyes widen, but he doesn't speak. Apparently, I've stunned the poor man into silence.

"Yes or no?" I ask. "Don't make me beg."

"No, I . . . *Yes*. I only paused because you're drunk. I don't want you to regret it tomorrow."

I press my forehead against his and smile. "Honey, I'm not *drunk,* I'm *buzzed*. Tipsy. Intoxicated enough to say the naughty things I want you to do to me out loud and sober enough to be certain it's not the booze talking."

Grayson laughs. "Okay, you've convinced me. Yes, I'll fuck you up your gorgeous ass."

I pat his head. "Atta boy."

Yet again, I can't help thinking how different I am with Grayson than Andre. My ex-husband used to beg me to perform this particular sex act, and I always said no. During our honeymoon, I said no because I simply didn't trust the motherfucker enough to let him do it. Even in those first days of our marriage, I was scared he'd hurt me—maybe even irrevocably. Talk about a red flag. After that, over time, I guess I also started enjoying the power trip of refusing him the one thing he wanted, above all else. By then, I was sick to death of sex with Andre always being about his pleasure and not mine. And since I figured anal sex would only be pleasant for *him,* literally nothing could convince me to give it a whirl.

But now with Grayson? I'm actually excited to try it. It's yet another green flag. Proof positive this relationship is everything I've been waiting for, without even realizing it.

"Did those Ball Peen Hammer videos you watched give any tips on anal?" I ask. "He's been your trusty wingman on everything else."

Grayson chuckles. "Actually, yeah, he definitely had a video on it. But it's been a while since I watched it." He scrunches up his face. "I think the main thing was, 'Be gentle and use lots of lube.'"

I grind my ass into his hard-on beneath me in the warm water. "Won't the hot water do the same thing as lube?" I gyrate my ass against Grayson's tip. "Plus, I'm really relaxed, thanks to the booze. I think we're good."

"Oh, God," Grayson whispers. Clearly, the lap dance I'm giving him is turning him on like crazy. "Better safe than sorry, though," he manages to say. "I don't want to risk hurting you."

The comment is so quintessentially Grayson, I can't help grabbing his face and planting a kiss on his mouth. "God, I love you." I kiss him again. "There's a bottle of lube in my nightstand. Will you grab it?"

"I'll be right back." He guides me off his lap and onto my ass next to him in the hot tub. "Drink the rest of this while I'm gone." He hands me a half-empty champagne flute from the ledge.

"Yes, sir."

Grayson climbs out of the hot tub and grabs a towel from a chair, prompting me to ogle his gorgeous body. He's always been hot to me, from day one. But since then, he's discovered a new passion for fitness, one that has slowly given him sculpted, lean muscles over the past six months. And the best part? Whenever I compliment Grayson on his new physique, he says something along the lines of "When a guy's got the hottest girlfriend in the world, he's got to do whatever he can to keep her coming back for more."

With his towel secured around his trim waist, Grayson bounds into my house to retrieve the lube. And when he returns a couple minutes later, he's got an extra-wide smile on his handsome face, a tent pole sticking out from behind his towel, and a little tube in his hand.

"Found it," he says.

"My ass is ready for you," I purr. I hold up my empty glass. "And my champagne is all gone." I've no sooner said the words than my beloved dog, Daisy, bounds through the sliding glass door left open by Grayson and tackles him.

"Aw, fuck," Grayson says. "No, Daisy!"

"She thinks it's a hot dog," I joke.

"Argh!" Grayson says. He grabs Daisy's collar and leads her back inside, muttering, "I don't want your puppy-dog eyes staring at me the whole time I'm fucking Mommy up the ass."

When Grayson returns, his dick is semi-flaccid. I stand and invite him back into the water, telling him I know exactly what to do to get him hard again.

He stands over me on the ledge and pointedly looks at my tits. And what do you know, his dick hardens right before my eyes.

"That's quite a magic trick," I say, laughing.

"It's not magic," he says. "It's Selena." With that, he slowly enters the hot tub, his massive erection leading the way. When he reaches me in the warm water, he pulls me into his strong arms and kisses me passionately. As his lips devour mine, I wrap my arms around Grayson's neck and rub my pelvis into his erection. For several minutes, we kiss and caress, our fingers exploring each other's bodies in the hot water. Until, finally, when we're both obviously extremely aroused, Grayson guides me to the ledge of the hot tub, turns me around, and tells me to place my palms on the ledge.

I feel his wet skin cleaving to my backside, so I push my ass into his hard-on, excited to feel him penetrating me in this whole new way. But he doesn't take the bait. Not yet. His mouth devours the crook of my neck while his wet fingers caress my breasts and pinch my hard nipples. When the tip of his cock invades the crack of my ass suggestively, my knees buckle with anticipation. Again and again, he teases me by pushing his cock in between my cheeks. But each time, he only rests his tip against my anus and doesn't push inside.

When my arousal reaches a fever pitch, I feel Grayson's body leave my backside. Hear the sound of lube being squirted out of a tube. And a moment later, Grayson slides his fingers up and down my ass crack, and then presses his fingertip against my anus, and then pushes his fingertip inside me.

"Do it," I mutter. "I'm ready."

"Don't hold your breath," Grayson whispers, his breath hot against my ear. "Breathe deeply."

I do as I'm told, and Grayson reaches around my torso and fondles my clit.

"Breathe," he reminds me, as his fingers explore my anus. "Breathe, my love. You're in full control. I'll go only as deep as you can handle."

I melt into the hot tub ledge. "I'm gonna come, if you keep touching me like this." I don't know if that's his goal—making me come before he's even taken the plunge into my backside—or if he's trying to bring me to the bitter edge before penetrating me. Either way, I'm a heartbeat away from coming undone.

I feel the sensation of my anus being stretched. Pressure. A sensation that makes me feel strangely like I'm gagging, even though that makes no sense.

"That's the tip," Grayson chokes out. "Oh, fuck."

"That feels okay," I manage to say. "Keep going."

"Breathe, baby. Take a deep breath."

I do as I'm told, and the next thing I know, I feel like my eyes are popping out of my head. "Holy fuck," I gasp out. "That's a lot."

"Pull out?"

"No. Just give me a minute. Are you all the way in?"

"About halfway." His voice is quavering. He sounds like he's holding on for dear life.

"Does it feel good to you?" I ask.

"Fucking amazing."

"Give me a minute to relax into it." I breathe deeply. "Oh, fuck."

"I can pull out."

"Don't you dare. We've come too far. Touch my clit again."

"Yes, MILF." He begins caressing my swollen clit, moving it in circles, and soon, I'm moaning softly and crumpling into the ledge of the hot tub.

"Open your legs," he chokes out. "Take another big breath."

I do as he's instructed, and suddenly, there's no doubt Grayson is all the way in. Or if not, he's as far in as my body will allow. He continues massaging my clit, while slowly thrusting—and, *bam!*—I'm suddenly feeling intense pleasure unlike anything I've felt before.

"Okay?" he chokes out, his voice strained.

"Yes. Oh my God. Don't go any faster, but don't stop."

Grayson continues gently moving inside me, while still fingering my clit. And the result is pure magic—lightning bolts of pleasure zapping nerve endings in previously unconquered territories. Indeed, with each passing minute, I'm feeling ever more drunk with pleasure.

I clutch the concrete ledge in front of me as a bolt of pure ecstasy slams me, which is then followed by an intense orgasm crashing through me. It's defying gravity, this orgasm. Shattering and warping me in ways that make me feel like I'm short-circuiting. Making every muscle flex and shudder at once.

With a roar, Grayson comes behind me—which I know to be the case, not only because of the sound he's making, but because I can feel his cock rippling violently inside me. I collapse onto the tub ledge and Grayson falls onto my back, spewing a stream of expletives.

We remain still for a long moment, with both of us breathing hard. And then Grayson drags my slack body to sit on the edge of the hot tub, at which point he begins voraciously eating my pussy . . . which, shockingly, brings me to orgasm, yet again, in less than a minute.

As my latest climax subsides, Grayson pulls my wet, sweaty, flopping body into the warm water and straight into his waiting arms, where I practically faint into his chest and babble incoherently.

Grayson holds me for a very long time—which is a very good thing, considering I've momentarily lost control of my limbs. "Come on, love," he finally says softly, his lips pressed to my ear. "We're going upstairs now. We're going to drink a gallon of water and take a long shower and crawl into bed. And when we wake up in the morning, I'm going to eat your pussy first thing, make you the best damned pancakes you've ever had while wearing nothing but an apron and a smile, and then eat your pussy again, this time on your kitchen table." He kisses my cheek. "Sound good?"

"Like heaven."

Grayson moves to help me out of the hot tub, but pauses, looking concerned. "Are you okay?"

I slump into his frame, press my forehead into the crook of his neck, and sigh happily. "My love, I'm fan-fucking-tastic."

17
GRAYSON

"Delicious," Selena says, before popping another bite of blueberry pancake into her mouth. We're sitting at her kitchen table in the late-morning sunshine, finishing off the breakfast made with love by yours truly. I'm wearing a kitchen apron and a smile, as promised last night. Selena is wearing black undies and a white tank top that accentuates her amazing tits and nipples. Which, of course, means my naked dick is currently rock-hard behind my apron.

"Tell me something, my darling," Selena says, narrowing her dark eyes. "Did you happen to swipe a pair of red undies from my hamper?"

"Red undies?"

"Mm hmm. When I gathered up my dirty laundry this morning, they were nowhere to be found, even though I'm sure I tossed them in there yesterday morning."

"How strange. 'The Case of the Disappearing Lace Panties.'"

"I never said they were lace."

I wink. "Just a guess."

Selena rolls her eyes. "Honey, there's no reason to steal my panties ever again. I've already invited you to stay here regularly —whenever Drew is at Andre's or a friend's house."

I lean forward and smirk. "But I got off on stealing them. I liked thinking I was getting away with something."

"Naughty boy."

"Plus, I only had that one pair from way back when—from our first long weekend together. I needed a fresh trophy to commemorate my very first night staying at your house. Last night was big for me."

"That's not the only thing that was 'big' about last night." She snickers. As silly as it is, Selena often makes jokes about my big dick, and I can't deny I fucking love it. "Seriously, though," she says, "How often are you planning to steal my undies, going forward? Every time you come over to my house? Only when you stay overnight? Do I need to start buying in bulk?"

I put down my coffee mug with a wink. "Maybe I'll start stealing your panties so often, you'll get so sick of needing to replace them, you'll invite me to stay overnight, even when Drew is home, if only to save yourself the hassle."

Selena giggles. "Silly man. Wouldn't you prefer to stay overnight more often because I'm emotionally ready to take that next step with you, rather than because you've worn me down by constantly pilfering my undergarments?"

"My love, I'll do whatever I have to do to get where I'm going. I'm relentless. A man on a mission."

She playfully arches an eyebrow. "I must admit, you're sexy when determined."

"And you're sexy when you breathe."

She laughs. Thankfully, she hasn't looked the least bit annoyed throughout this entire exchange, even though I've now impliedly revealed my not-so-secret endgame: to one day live here with her. To be her life partner. To never have to sleep another night alone in my bed, away from her. As far as I'm concerned, Selena can take all the time she needs to get there with me. Contrary to what I just said, I do, in fact, only want her to invite me to live with her when she's ready to take that step. But she looks so receptive to this line of playful banter, I can't help pushing the envelope a bit to discover where her current limits might be.

"Careful what you wish for, Grayson-hopper," Selena says flirtatiously. "Thus far, you've only seen a curated version of me. I'm the woman who shows up for our dates in a glamorous puff of smoke, fulfills all your fantasies—"

"And then some."

"And then disappears for a few days, always leaving you wanting more."

"Always. I want it all, baby."

"So you think. But the only thing you're missing out on, really, is the boring stuff. When I'm not with you, I'm doing laundry and grocery shopping. I'm sitting in my office for hours on end, working hard. I'm going to Drew's various games and shuttling him around."

I put down my mug. "Okay, you've convinced me. it. I could never be with someone who does laundry and shuttles a kid and sits in her office for hours on end, working hard. Jesus. You're a monster."

She rolls her eyes. "All I'm saying is that, as we move into this next phase of our relationship, we should take it slow, in case whatever new information we both discover creates any hiccups. I'm not always as fun as I am when I'm around you, Grayson. In my real life, I get stressed out. Cranky. Sometimes, I get pissed at Drew for not doing his chores or leaving food out in the kitchen. I get frazzled about deadlines for work."

"Monster."

"Oh, and I get horrible menstrual cramps the first day of my period and only want to stay in bed all day with a heating pad, watching rom coms."

"I like rom coms."

"The point is we need to take this at a pace that leaves room for both of us to discover and acclimate to whatever unexpected character traits or flaws we don't yet know about."

I exhale. "Okay. All that stuff you mentioned—grocery shopping and laundry and shuttling Drew around? It's the stuff I physically *crave* to do with you, every bit as much as I crave to eat your pussy."

Selena furrows her brow and flashes me a look of incredulity.

"Okay, *almost* as much."

She laughs. "Let's keep things real, sweetheart. No bullshitting at this table allowed."

I lean back in my chair. "You want to keep things real?"

"I do. I want full honesty."

"Okay." I choose my words for a long moment. "Whatever you need to do to feel good about taking the next step with me—which to me would mean making this relationship a full-blown, full-time, lifelong partnership without limitations or compartmentalization—then that's great with me. If I hurry or pressure you, if I push you to go faster than you're ready to do, then this relationship won't work out in the end. So, that'd be a stupid move on my part. I'm well aware that *slowly* is the fastest way to get where I want to be."

Her features melt. "You're a diehard romantic, Grayson McKnight."

"And you're not."

"No, I'm not. I'm in love with you. I'm the luckiest woman alive to have found you. But please don't tie all your happiness to the word 'forever' just yet. Let's take it a day at a time and enjoy this amazing love we feel for each other while we continue to learn even more about each other."

I lean back in my chair. "Cool."

"Don't forget, I've got Drew to consider, and he's already got enough chaos in his life."

I nod. "I haven't forgotten. I know your life has far more moving parts than mine."

"If I had nothing but my own heart to consider, I'd probably invite you stay with me, every night of the week. Honestly, I physically ache whenever I'm away from you. I've never been happier than I was when I woke up this morning in my bed and saw your face on the next pillow."

My heart feels like it's expanding to twice its size. "I swear, if I thought you'd say yes, I'd ask you to marry me right now."

She gasps. "*Grayson.*"

Fuck. I can't believe I just said that. What's wrong with me? The woman is in the middle of giving me a speech about taking things slowly, and I decided now was the right time to bring up marriage?

"Sorry," I whisper. "I shouldn't have said that."

Selena's face is flushed. She swallows hard. "Was it the truth?"

I take a deep breath. "Yes. Absolutely. If I was sure you'd say yes to me, I'd ask you to marry me right now and run off to City Hall to do the deed this afternoon."

Thank God, she's smiling.

"Although, actually, if I'm being completely honest, I wouldn't need to be sure you'd say yes before asking you. If I thought there was even a sliver of a chance you'd say yes, I'd probably ask you. Better that, than wondering 'What if?' When I played Little League as a kid, I always swung for the fences, rather than trying to hit a single."

She giggles. "And did you ever hit a homer?"

"No. Not once."

"Aw."

"Actually, I wound up with the worst batting average on the team. But I kept trying. Every. Fucking. Time."

Her dark eyes are sparkling. Her cheeks are rosy. She's thoroughly amused by this anecdote. In fact, everything about her body language tells me she's feeling particularly enamored with me right now. So, fuck it. On a whim, I decide to swing for the fences, the same way I always did as a kid.

I take her hand. "Selena Diaz, will you marry me?"

Her mouth hangs open, and I know I've shocked the living shit out of her.

I squeeze her hand and release her. "This isn't an ultimatum. You said, 'No bullshit,' so I'm merely laying all my cards on the table. One day, I want to have some kind of forever with you. Am I thrilled I finally get to spend the night here with you? Absolutely. It was the best night of my life. Was it amazing to get to meet Drew? Hell yes. Even when he made fun of me. But do I want more at some point? Fuck yes, I do. I want it all. Because I already know you're The One. Because I love you more than life. Because every night away from you is pure torture." I grin. "And if I'm being brutally honest with you without holding back, the idea of you doing laundry gives me a raging hard-on."

She laughs. "Everything I do gives you a raging hard-on."

"That's literally my entire point."

She's glowing. "Speaking of laundry, I won't be doing yours. I don't even do Drew's anymore. When you stay here, you'll have to fend for yourself in that department. I'm not your maid or your mommy."

My heart is pounding. I have to think her negotiating the terms of my overnight stays at her house is a good sign. "Of course, I'll do my own laundry. You're my Hot Teacher. My hot MILF. My hot girlfriend. If anyone's gonna be doing anyone else's laundry around here, then I'll be doing yours."

Selena fans herself. "That was the hottest thing you've ever said to me, Grayson-hopper. Amen to that. Keep saying stuff like that to me, and I might start throwing my lace panties at you and begging you to steal them." As I laugh, she chews on the inside of her cheek, her brown eyes dancing. She asks, "When does the lease expire on your apartment?"

I can't believe she's asking me this question. Is she considering asking me to live here with her and Drew after my lease expires? I clear my throat. I can barely breathe. "I renewed the lease a couple months ago. Two or three months ago, I think."

"For a year?" When I nod, she processes that for a beat. "Okay, love," she says. "Here's what I think we should do. For now, we'll take our relationship slowly, one day at a time, and not think too much about this future of chores and normalcy you're envisioning. We'll take some time to get to know each other in a whole new way. You and Drew will get to know each other, too. And we'll meet each other's parents. And if, by the time your lease ends, things are still going the way they are now, only better, if we simply can't stand spending a single night apart by then, and everything still feels natural and right, despite all the new people and boring stuff we've brought into our little bubble, then we'll sit down and talk about you not renewing that lease . . . and living here. Full-time."

My heart feels like it's exploding. "That sounds fucking fantastic."

She exhales with relief. "You're honestly okay with that timeline?"

"Absolutely."

"Phew. I was worried you'd say I'm moving too slowly for you."

I shrug. "If I'm being honest, I think things will happen more quickly than you're anticipating. Just a hunch. But I promise I'll never pressure you. Like I said, this is your house, your rules."

"Thank you so much."

"I do have one question, though, before we leave this topic. Just to be clear, is your answer no to marrying me? You never gave me an answer."

Selena snorts. But then, she says something surprising. "I wouldn't say my answer is no. It's more like 'Patience, Grayson-hopper. We're not there *yet*.'"

I can't believe my ears. I lean my forearms onto the kitchen table, brimming with optimism and excitement. "Well, in that case, I've got a proposed amendment to the plan you've laid out. I promise I won't think about the future, as you've requested —*except* for when I'm periodically asking you to marry me, at which point we'll both agree I'm allowed to momentarily indulge my romanticism, ever so briefly, and think about the future I'm dying to have with you."

Selena tilts her head. "What, exactly, do you mean by 'periodically'?"

I shrug. "Once a week?"

Selena scoffs. "That'd be insane. No. That's way too often, Grayson."

"Not when I'd want to ask you twice a day. And we'd still be doing things your way, all other days of the week. All I'm asking is you give me a tiny window each week to swing for the fences."

She shakes her head. "It's too often for me, but also for you. I can't let you do that to yourself, honey. I'm not going to change my mind, from one week to the next. Which means you'll start feeling like you're banging your head against a brick wall. You'll feel hurt and rejected, instead of energized and optimistic. What would be the point in that?"

"I won't feel rejected, if I propose to you the same way I just did. That was fun, wasn't it?"

"It was," she concedes.

"So, I'll ask you like that, once a week. I'll keep it casual.

No pressure. I'll do it at the breakfast table, just like today. Or maybe I'll do it at night in bed, just to keep you guessing. The point is there'll be no grand gestures. No tension. It'll always be nothing but light-hearted and fun—my way of letting you know my feelings and dreams haven't changed. God willing, you'll reply with 'Patience, Grayson-hopper, we're not there *yet*,' and I'll know you're not saying 'no' or 'never.' That will be enough hope to keep me feeling optimistic." I grin. "Hope is sunshine, soil, and water to a little seedling like me, Hot Teacher."

Selena looks surprisingly serious. She processes my speech for a long moment, before finally surprising me with, "Once a month. That's my final offer."

I can't believe it. She's actually agreeing to this lunacy? Quickly, before she can take it back, I say "deal" and take her hand.

"And if it stops being fun for you," she says, shaking my hand. "If you realize your feelings have started to get hurt, promise me you'll stop doing it."

I kiss the top of her hand and release it. "Not likely, but okay. I promise."

"Good."

I swallow hard, unsure if I should say the thing on the tip of my tongue. Finally, I decide to go for it. "On the flipside, if one day you realize you're actually ready to say yes to me the next time I propose, could you please let me know that? Not with explicit words, necessarily. I'm not asking you to propose to me. But maybe you could give me some kind of heads-up or smoke signal to let me know you've had that epiphany? That way, I'll know to make my next proposal a proper one with all the bells and whistles."

Selena does that thing where she looks at me like I'm adorably naïve. But, come on, none of this should surprise her. From our first meeting at Captain's, she knew I'd fall hard and fast for her. She said so herself. Well, here I am: more in love with her than I ever thought possible.

"And what if I've realized I love you with all my heart and want you to live here with me as my partner but not as my husband?" she asks. "What if I realize I don't want to get married again to anyone, not even to you? If I have that realization, I'm going to have to tell you that, too, Grayson."

"Well, fuck yeah, you'd better tell me that, or else I'm going to cluelessly keep asking my girlfriend to marry me till I'm one-hundred-and-three."

Selena chuckles. "You're a very silly man, Grayson McKnight."

"Honestly, if you said that to me, if you said you're not willing to get married again, I'd be okay with that, as long as you still wanted *me*. I've never believed marriage is a requirement for a happy life. As long as I've got you, I'll always be happy. You're all I need, forever."

She looks skeptical. "If that's the case, then why ask me to marry you at all?"

"Because it's romantic and fun and I'd love to be your husband. So, why not? I'm just saying it's not a deal-breaker for me. I'm not going anywhere, no matter what we call our relationship."

Selena touches the top of my hand. "You're such a darling romantic."

My heart flutters. "So, do we have a deal? We'll do things your way and take things slow for the next year or so, except for once a month when I'll swing for the fences and ask you to marry me—and you won't freak out when I do that, because you'll know there's no pressure and it's all in good fun. All part of my master plan of wearing you down. Except, of course, that I'll be totally serious, each and every time I ask you, so you're always welcome to give me a 'yes' any ol' time you're feeling it—but a heads-up would be appreciated."

She takes a deep breath and exhales. "We've got a deal, except that I need you to promise you'll stop asking me, if it's no longer fun for you."

"Deal." I rise, revealing the erection that's poking out from behind the fabric of my apron. "Now, come here, goddess. Let me seal this deal by giving you a squirting orgasm all over your kitchen table."

18

GRAYSON

"*You Can't Hurry Love.*"

That's the song blaring in Selena's kitchen—yet another hit from the "60's Hits" playlist Selena put on for her father's birthday dinner.

Selena is standing at her stove, stirring something in a pan. I'm mincing garlic to her left at the kitchen counter. Her father and Drew are playing Scrabble behind us at a table.

As the simple, happy song blares, Selena is dancing in place at the stove. I stop working on the garlic to watch her. Is this playlist one of those ready-made ones offered by the streaming platform, or did Selena personally select tonight's tunes? If it's the latter scenario, then I wouldn't be surprised if Selena specifically chose this song as a coded message to me. At this point, I've lost track of how many times she's answered one of my marriage proposals with "Patience, Grayson-hopper." Surely, it's not paranoia to think she might have chosen this song to reinforce the usual messaging.

As I'm watching Selena bopping along to the music at the stove, she turns to look at me. When our eyes meet, she begins pointedly singing along to the song's chorus, like she's intentionally serenading me with those specific lyrics. Well, that settles it. Whether she selected this song or not, she's now using it to remind me about the fine art of patience.

True to my word, I've kept my monthly proposals fun and casual these past nine months, and Selena's always made it clear she's not the least bit annoyed or freaked out. In fact, thanks to the white-hot sex that always follows one of my monthly proposals, there's not a doubt in my mind Selena genuinely gets off on being asked.

But lately, I can't deny I'm beginning to look for that heads-up she promised to give me, if she ever started to feel ready to say yes. I didn't bother looking for one during the first six months of our little arrangement. Each time I asked, I knew she'd turn me down. But for the last few months, I've started to feel a shift in Selena. A readiness to take things to the next level. So now, I must admit I'm not only on the constant look-out for that heads-up from her, I'm yearning for it.

I can't fathom why Selena *wouldn't* feel ready to say yes to me at this point. First of all, she gets along fantastically well with my mother. I thought it would be weird between the two women, since my mother is only seven years older than Selena. But no. They clicked from the start. Also, Drew and I have become extremely close. So much so, Drew often invites me over, even when his mother is off at a client dinner or something. As a result, Selena started letting me spend the night here months ago, even on nights when Drew is home. And I've been a fixture at weekly family dinners with Selena's father, whom I call Pops, for several months now.

Speaking of Pops, he suddenly blurts "Ha!" behind me, so I turn around to see what's up. Based on body language, it's apparent he's made a great play in his game of Scrabble with Drew, so I ask him what word he laid down, and off he goes excitedly explaining his prowess to me.

Midway through his explanation, however, the song blaring

through Selena's kitchen switches to a new one that quickly commands my full attention. I turn back around to look at Selena at the stove to my right—and quickly realize this song is most definitely an intentional, coded message to me. In fact, *hallelujah*, I think it could be the smoke signal I've been waiting for!

The song is "Going to the Chapel." And when I look at Selena, she's singing along pointedly to the lyrics with a huge smile on her face. Everything about Selena's facial expression and body language as she sings about going to the chapel to get married practically screams, *This is on purpose! This is planned! Listen up!* And suddenly, there's no doubt she's telling me she's *finally* ready to say yes to me—to go to the chapel with me—or the beach or City Hall—and get ma-a-arried.

With my heart crashing in my ears and a massive grin on my face to match Selena's, I watch the love of my life serenading me at the stove. When the last chorus begins, she glides toward me, slides her arms around my neck, and softly sings the remainder of the simple song into my ear.

When the music ends, Selena kisses my cheek and whispers, "I love you with all my heart and soul, Grayson McKnight. Forever and always. Without holding back. And I'll never change my mind about that, as long as I live."

The boner that's been thickening in my pants hardens to steel, as my heart bursts with joy. This is the best moment of my life, by far. The answer to my prayers. I pull Selena into me, gently press my palms against her cheeks, and kiss her mouth. Selena's typically not a fan of PDA, other than holding hands. And that's especially true when we're in the presence of her father and kid. But, clearly, usual preferences don't apply in a euphoric, life-changing moment like this. A moment this amazing and unique—a once in a lifetime moment like this—surely calls for a deep and passionate kiss.

As I kiss my future wife, she not only doesn't pull away, she presses herself against me and returns my kiss with everything she has. It's how I know, for sure, I'm not crazy. I'm not engaging in wishful thinking. *Selena Diaz wants to become my wife.*

"I love you, too," I whisper into her ear. "Forever and always. With all my heart and soul. And I'll never change my mind about that, as long as I live."

She kisses my cheek, reaches around and pats my ass, and then returns to her pan on her stove, like she didn't just rock my entire fucking world.

The playlist has now moved on to its next song—a tune I don't recognize. Drew and Pops are still cluelessly playing Scrabble at the table. The clock on the wall continues its ticking march. But the world is forever changed for me. The next time I ask Selena to marry me, she's going to say *yes*.

"Hey, sous chef," Selena calls to me. "Where's that minced garlic?"

I clear my throat. "I got distracted by a smoke signal."

She giggles. "How lovely. But I need that garlic. Chop, chop. Literally."

"Yes, MILF." *Oops.* I know better than to use that nickname for Selena around her son and father. A bit louder, I add, "Yes, *ma'am*." I glance over my shoulder to see if Pops and Drew overheard my first version, and thankfully, it seems they didn't. I quickly finish my mincing job and slide my work into Selena's pan.

"Nice work," she says with a wink. "It needs to simmer for five and then I'll let it sit to thicken for another five. And then, finally, we'll feast." She calls to her father at the kitchen table. "Dinner's ready in ten, Dad. Should I open another bottle of that same red for you?"

He glances at his empty goblet. "Absolutely. I'm drinking only the good stuff on my birthday."

Selena addresses me. "Would you grab another bottle from the wine cellar?"

"You bet." As I cross the kitchen, I feel like I'm floating on air. *I'm going to marry Selena Diaz. Holy fucking shit.*

Right before I've reached the kitchen table, Pops happens to get up in front of me, murmuring something about hitting the bathroom before dinnertime. And that's when I realize the perfect opportunity has fallen into my lap.

I hang back and stalk Pops as he disappears into a nearby bathroom and then wait outside the door, fidgeting and thinking about the speech I'm going to give him when he comes out. I choose and re-choose my words in my head, feeling increasingly excited and anxious. And when the man finally emerges from the bathroom, I'm horrified to hear myself blurt, with zero preamble or finesse, "May I have your blessing to marry Selena?"

Fuck.

That's not how I was planning to do that. I was planning to slowly ramp up to the ultimate request.

Selena's father stops short outside the bathroom door and stares at me for a beat. Calmly, he says, "I think perhaps we should talk about this a bit farther away from the kitchen, don't you?"

"Yes, sir. Good thinking."

I follow him into the family room, and we both take seats—with Pops taking an imposing armchair and me sinking into the leather couch across from him.

"Now, tell me what's on your mind, Grayson," he says as he crosses his ankle onto his knee.

I take a deep breath. "Sir, I love your daughter with all my heart and soul, and nothing will ever change that. I'm planning to ask her to marry me, and I'd very much like to get your blessing before doing that, if you'd honor me with it." *Whew.*

That was a lot more like the speech I practiced in my head outside the bathroom door. Not perfect. But not too shabby, either.

The man smiles. "Haven't you already asked Selena to marry you several times, without first asking for my blessing? So, why ask me now?"

Shit. Why didn't I realize Selena would tell her beloved father about all those prior proposals? Those two are tight as ticks, and Selena's clearly enjoyed all of them.

"Those were practice runs, basically, meant to let Selena know how serious I am about her. Also, I think I've been trying to normalize the idea for her—you know, inching her closer and closer to feeling like saying yes to me one day wouldn't be the craziest thing in the world to do."

"Do *you* think it would be crazy for her to marry you?"

"Uh. No. I . . . I think I misspoke. I meant I've been normalizing the idea for *her*; in case *she* thinks it'd be a crazy thing to do. I don't think it'd be crazy at all. Honestly, I've been hoping she'll one day feel ready to say yes to me for a very long time."

"And you think that day is finally here?"

"Yes, I do, sir." I explain the whole thing to him, concluding with the fact that Selena pointedly serenaded me in the kitchen a few minutes ago with a highly suggestive song. "And she didn't correct or contradict me when I told her I'd gotten distracted by a 'smoke signal,'" I say in conclusion. "In fact, when I specifically used that phrase—smoke signal—she replied only with, 'How lovely.' Not 'You misunderstood me, Grayson.' I think that's a pretty good indication she was confirming my interpretation of events, don't you?"

Pops returns my wide grin. "It sure seems like it."

I shudder with excitement. "I'm positive Selena was telling me it's finally time to propose to her for real, sir. It's time for me to pull out all the stops and give her the kind of proposal she deserves, with all the bells and whistles. And that includes getting your blessing, if you're willing to give it to me."

Pops leans back into his chair and steeples his fingers. "And if I'm not?"

My stomach sinks. "I'll ask her, anyway. Nothing will stop me. But I'd strongly prefer to have your blessing, because I know how much Selena values your opinion."

My heart is galloping as the man ponders my comments for what feels like an eternal moment. Finally, he says, "Grayson, my daughter has been married and divorced. She's a grown woman with a teenaged son and a successful business. At this point, I don't feel qualified to tell her what to do in any aspect of her life—least of all, in her love life. Let's not forget, I'm the fucking idiot who gave Andre my blessing, way back when, and I couldn't have been more wrong to do that."

"I'm not Andre," I say quickly. "I hope that's abundantly clear to you, sir. I'll never hurt Selena. Never."

He looks sympathetic. "I believe that, Grayson. You're a loyal, faithful, gentle soul, if I've ever met one. And it's obvious your love for my daughter is genuine. All I'm saying is, at this stage of my daughter's life, I don't think I should have any say in what she decides to do with her heart. As her father, I'll always want what's best for her. I'll always try to guide and protect her, as best I can, of course. But her decisions are all hers."

"Yes, sir. I can respect that."

He smiles. "That said, if my daughter decides she wants to marry you, then I'd not only fully support her decision, I'd also be thrilled about it."

I exhale an ocean of relief, lurch out of my chair, and begin shaking his hand enthusiastically. "Thank you, sir. I promise I'll always—"

"Assuming you'll agree to signing an ironclad prenup, that is."

I release his hand. "Of course. I don't want a dime of Selena's money."

Pops retakes my hand with a chuckle and pats it. "I know that. I'm simply informing you, if Selena were to ask her father for advice, that's what I'd advise her: to get a prenup. But, of course, I'd also congratulate my daughter on finding a kind man who'll love and treat her right."

Again, I exhale. "Thank you, sir. I'll sign anything. Do anything. I want a life with Selena and Drew that has nothing to do with her money or yours. I'll pay her rent to live here with her, if that's what she wants. I'll—"

He chuckles. "Stop, Grayson. I know you love Selena for all the right reasons. You can stop hard selling me now."

"Yes, sir."

"And, please. Don't offer to pay her rent. You want to be her husband, not her tenant, right?"

"Yes, sir. Thank you, sir. That was a stupid thing to say. I'm nervous."

"Don't be. You've got this."

"Dinner's ready!" Selena calls from the kitchen. "Where is everybody?"

"Go on now," Pops says with a wink. "Go get that bottle of that red I like so much and hurry back."

"Yes, sir. Gladly. Thank you, sir. So much."

"No need to call me sir, Grayson. Call me Pops. I like it when you call me that."

Oh, my heart. "Yes, sir! I mean, Pops!" I turn to sprint away, feeling like I've got a jetpack on my back, but stop when Selena's father calls to me.

"Get a really good bottle of champagne, too, son," he says behind me. When I stop and look at him, he adds, "Sounds like we've got a lot to celebrate tonight."

"Oh, I'm not going to ask her *tonight*. I need to get a ring and figure out my game plan. I want it to be extra-special for her, the next time I ask."

"Get some champagne, anyway. If you're right and Selena really did give you a 'smoke signal' in the kitchen earlier, then I want to secretly celebrate something even more exciting than my birthday tonight."

19
GRAYSON

I rise from my chair as Max approaches our corner table in the restaurant. Back when I worked at the law firm, I used to see Max all the time. These days, however, with all the various demands on my time and Max's, I don't see him as often as I'd like. In fact, it's been months since we've been able to catch up.

"Great to see you," I say enthusiastically, bro-hugging Max and patting his back.

"You, too." Max looks me up and down. "Holy shit, Gray, you're looking fit!"

We take our seats.

"Thanks. You look in top shape, as usual."

"Meh," Max replies. "I've been eating like shit and working too hard to get into the gym as much as I'd like. Thank God for my fast metabolism." He visibly ogles me from across the table. "What the fuck have you been doing at the gym? Whatever it is, teach me."

I laugh. "It's nothing special. Just consistency, I guess. Selena's got a killer home gym, so I'm able to squeeze in daily workouts, no matter the weird hour."

Max picks up his menu. "If we were still going out to bars together, you could be *my* wingman these days. You certainly wouldn't get any more fake numbers, that's for sure."

I shake my head. "If I get my way, I'll never ask another woman for her phone number, as long as I live."

Max chuckles. "Things are going that well with Selena?"

"Couldn't be better."

"When I first saw you, I thought she must have dumped you. Guys always work out hardest after a bad breakup."

"Nope. The happier I get, the more I feel like working out. Plus, I take my job as Selena's arm candy seriously."

Max laughs. "Whatever's motivating you, it's working. So, I take it you're living at Selena's place now, based on your daily workouts in her gym?"

"Not officially. I still have my apartment and sleep there once or twice a week—usually, when Selena's going to be out late with a client or her son."

"Oh, I forgot she's got a kid. How old is he?"

"Fourteen."

"Is it weird having him around?"

"Not at all. We're buddies. Drew texts me all the time. We watch movies and play video games. He beats me in basketball in his driveway. Sometimes, I play Dungeons & Dragons with him and his friends. He even asks me to come over when Selena's not around."

"Whoa. That's intense."

"It's awesome."

A waiter arrives and places some chips, salsa, and waters on the table. He takes our drink orders and says he'll return soon to take our food orders.

As the waiter leaves, Max peruses his menu. "So, what's good here, Gray?"

"Everything. You can't go wrong."

"Well, that narrows it down." He studies his menu for a long moment and finally puts it down, murmuring something about fish tacos. "It's so weird for me to think you're best buds with Andre De La Torre's kid and dating his wife. I never saw that one coming. Not in a million years."

"His *ex*-wife. And I'm not *dating* Selena. I'm going to marry that woman."

Max snickers. "Yeah, but let's not forget Andre is a fucking psychopath. Or at least, a sociopath. If I were you, I'd sleep with a baseball bat at my bedside every time I stayed the night at Selena's house, just in case Andre suddenly gets a wild hair up his ass about his former employee regularly fucking the mother of his child."

I take a sip of my water. I thought I was dropping a bombshell by revealing my intention to marry Selena, but it's clear Max thought it was nothing but a figure of speech. The sort of thing guys often say hyperbolically after meeting an amazing woman who seems too good to be true.

"Fuck Andre," I say. "He's a flea on an elephant's ass. Not even worth thinking about."

I'm a liar. In truth, I think about Andre all the time. First off, because Drew still goes to his father's house half the week, so I get to hear about his adventures whenever he returns home to Selena and me.

But even more than that, I find myself thinking about Andre in a totally different context, too, far more often than I'd care to admit. I hate the fact that Andre, who treated Selena like shit through twelve years of marriage, will forever hold the sacred and esteemed title of "Selena's former *husband*," while a guy who worships the ground she walks on and would take a bullet for her has so far been relegated to being introduced at parties as her "boyfriend." I understand the situation, intellectually. The disparity between Andre and me, in terms of status. But in my own head, especially if I've been drinking, when I think about

Andre being Selena's ex-*husband,* I want to pummel the life force right out of him.

Max pops a chip into his mouth. "Ha. If you ever did marry Selena, Andre would lose his motherfucking shit. Divorced or not, he's the kind of guy who thinks every cookie he's ever licked eternally belongs to him."

"Well, first off, Andre has never been a fan of licking cookies. Apparently, he's always found that particular sex act 'boring' and 'beneath him.'"

Max gasps. "*What?*"

I nod. "Selena said Andre was a horrible lover. Selfish as shit. Never even tried to get her off. It was always all about him."

"What the actual fuck?"

"It makes sense, though, right? But I digress. The more important thing I want to tell you is this." I reach into my pocket, pull out a closed ring box, and plunk it onto the table next to the basket of chips. "If me proposing to Selena will make Andre lose his motherfucking shit, then he'd better get ready to lose it. Because earlier when I said I'm going to marry Selena, it wasn't a figure of speech."

I flip open the box with flair to reveal the massive rock I've purchased for Selena, and Max's jaw nearly clanks onto the table.

"Holy fuck!" Max whisper-shouts, his eyes like saucers. "Is that thing *real?*"

I nod. "Only the best for Selena."

Max leans back in his seat, visibly flabbergasted. "Please tell me your new company is taking off like crazy and you didn't take out a loan to buy that rock for her."

I suppress the urge to smirk. As a matter of fact, my new company is killing it. So much so, I'm now probably making four times Max's salary as a high-priced lawyer—and I'm just getting started. Thanks to my ownership stake in the company, my net worth will probably be in the tens of millions in five years or so—maybe even in the *hundreds* of millions, if we wind up getting acquired by one of the heavy hitters that's recently been sniffing around.

But there's no reason to tell Max any of that. Instead, I'm perfectly content to let my buddy think he's the bigger baller at this table. He's the one who attended years of law school and is currently in student loan hell to the tune of hundreds of thousands of dollars. He's the one who works weekends and hasn't had the time or bandwidth to ask anyone on a second date in years. So, why not let him think he's winning at the game of life, in comparison to me, at least in terms of the trajectories of our bank accounts?

"Yeah, my company's doing great," I reply. "But we're a start-up, you know, so most of our revenue gets reinvested back into the company." It's true, although my bank account is nonetheless flush beyond my wildest dreams from mere distributions alone.

Max makes a sympathetic clicking noise with his mouth. "Start-ups can be rough. Hang in there. It's a marathon, not a sprint."

"Thanks. That's good advice." I motion to the small box on the table. "Thankfully, I had some money put away for a condo when I first met Selena. But with the way things have been going, I figured I'd much rather use that money to buy a 'condo' for Selena's finger."

Max chuckles. "A 'condo' is right. Damn, boy. That's the kind of rock pro athletes and moguls give to their women. She's going to freak out when she sees that thing."

I click the box closed when I notice the waiter approaching our table. "Let's hope so."

The waiter sets down our drinks—a margarita for me and a beer for Max—and we order our food. As he walks away, Max says, "Have you decided how you're going to pop the question?"

"I'm still figuring that out. I want to pull out all the stops this time. No more fucking around."

Max's eyebrows shoot up. "'This time?' Have you proposed to her before?"

I blush. "Lots of times, actually."

Max can't believe it. "And she's said no to you, each and every time?"

I explain the whole thing. "But now," I say in conclusion, "the time is finally here for me to pull out all the stops and give her the kind of fairytale proposal she deserves. No more hot tubs or proposals at breakfast. This time will be the real deal. I even asked her dad for his blessing the other night."

Max gasps. "Did he give it to you?"

"Sort of."

I relay the gist of what Selena's father said to me, and Max hoots with laughter.

"Now, *that's* a badass father!" he says.

"He's the best."

Max holds up his beer and clinks my glass. "Well, here's hoping you finally get that yes, my friend. I'm rooting for you."

"Thanks. Amen."

After a bit, the waiter arrives with our food—fish tacos for Max and a burrito for me—and we proceed to dig in while chatting about some big patent case Max has been working on. Now that I no longer work for the law firm, I can't imagine he's still allowed to tell me this stuff. But Max doesn't seem to care about that technicality, so I don't stop him from talking. After a while, though, Max returns the conversation to my upcoming proposal. Specifically, to him giving me ideas for how to do it.

"Oh! You could whisk her away to a tropical vacation," Max suggests. "Ask her on the beach at sunset. That's sort of textbook 'romantic proposal,' isn't it?"

"Yeah, I was thinking of doing something like that. We're going to see my college buddy in LA in a few weeks. I was thinking I might book a suite at a fancy hotel in Santa Monica or Malibu and do it on our first night there."

Max slams his palm on the table, clearly having an epiphany. "You should ask her at your birthday party. All her family and friends will be there, right? You could turn your birthday party into an engagement party!"

I purse my lips. "Meh. I don't think so. Selena's a private person. I don't think she'd want me to ask her in front of a crowd." I pick up my margarita. "Are you coming to my party, by the way? I don't think we heard back from you."

"Oh, yeah, sorry. I've been working long hours. Forgot to RSVP. I'm coming—especially if it means I'll get to see Selena's reaction to that goddamned boulder of a ring."

I put down my glass. "I really don't think I'll do it at the party. Selena's not a fan of 'public proposals.'" I tell Max the story of the time, a few weeks ago, Selena and I took Drew to a Supersonics game and some guy got down on bended knee at center court during half-time. I explain that, after the proposal, Drew said something like, "Why do guys always propose in front of total strangers? I'd never do that. What if the woman says no?" And that Selena agreed with her son, saying, "I'm always worried the woman is going to do exactly that—say no and embarrass the poor guy in front of the world. Or, worse, that she'll say yes in the moment to save him from public humiliation, and then break his heart later on, in private."

Sitting across from me now, Max furrows his brow. He asks, "So, are you saying you're afraid Selena will publicly humiliate you? Or maybe say yes to you in the moment and then break your heart later on?"

My heart squeezes at the thought of either scenario. But what I say is, "Neither. Selena's going to say yes to me this time. Like I said, she gave me that 'smoke signal.' All I'm saying is I don't think she'd like a public proposal, and I want to make the proposal as perfect for her as possible."

Max scoffs. "Well, I wouldn't equate a party with good friends and family to a public basketball game, but, whatever. You're the one who knows her and what she'd like."

I ruminate on that for a moment and realize Max might be onto something here. Am I scared of public humiliation? I'm ninety-nine percent sure Selena will say yes when I ask her this next time, but I also know life is unpredictable and people change their minds about important things. Plus, I'm sometimes flat-out dumb when it comes to reading social cues. All of which means there's probably at least a one percent chance that Selena could turn me down this next time around, despite the heads-up she gave me in her kitchen last week. And if that were to happen, if she were to reject me again, would I want her son and father and everyone we know to witness my humiliation? Uh, no.

"Hey, don't stress it," Max says. Clearly, he's reacting to whatever he sees on my face. "She gave you a smoke signal, remember? You've got this, brother, no matter how you decide to do it." He smiles. "Gray, I was there when you met her for the first time, remember? And no offense, but you were a total fucking dork. Despite that fact, however—or maybe because of it—she wanted to leave the bar with you. She wanted to spend the whole weekend, screwing you. And she hasn't wanted to leave your side, ever since. Obviously, no matter how you ask her, or how badly you might think you're screwing it up, you're still going to sweep her off her feet. Because you're *you*."

I feel my cheeks turning red. "Thanks, Max. That was a surprisingly good pep talk."

Max grabs his drink. "I'm a lawyer, dude. I get paid big bucks to spew a load of bullshit and make it sound like I believe every word."

"Oh."

"Just kidding. I meant every word. You've got this."

I clink his drink with mine. "Well, whether that speech was

bullshit or not, it's given me the confidence to go with my initial idea. I'm gonna book a fancy suite during our trip to LA in a couple weeks, take her on a romantic walk at sunset, and surprise her with a string quartet playing 'Going to the Chapel' on the sand. While the music is playing and the waves are crashing, I'll get down on bended knee, pull out that whopper of a ring, and ask the most amazing woman in the world to be my wife."

Max can't help chuckling. "Damn, Gray. You've put some real thought into this. That's a damned good plan."

I exhale with relief. "You think?"

"It's perfect. Not even the slightest bit dorky."

"Then that's what I'll do." I bite my lip. "Should I hire an airplane to fly by, right as I'm kneeling down? I was thinking it could fly a banner that says, 'Marry me, Pulchritudinous Goddess!'"

Max chortles. "And . . . the dork is back."

"She'll like it. Trust me."

"Nix the plane, Gray. That's too many moving parts with timing and everything. Plus, you said she's private, right? You're already pushing it to have four musicians standing there when you ask her."

"Yeah, you're right. Thanks."

"Sure thing."

"But otherwise, the plan is solid gold, right?"

"It's diamond-encrusted platinum, baby."

I raise my drink, yet again, and we clink. "Thanks, brother. You want to be my best man?"

"Fuck yes."

"Awesome. Thanks." My cheeks hurt from smiling. "I'm so glad you helped me figure this out. This proposal will be the one Selena tells her father and Drew about. And all her friends, too. God help me, when everyone asks how I popped the question to her, I want Selena to feel proud of the story she tells them."

20

GRAYSON

My 27th birthday bash in the summer sunshine of Selena's sprawling backyard is in full swing—and hot damn, this birthday party's bumping! The DJ hired by Selena is perfect—fun and upbeat without being cheesy. The catered barbeque is delicious, while the specialty cocktails, including "The Grey Goose Grayson"—all drinks prepared by a smiling, professional bartender—are a huge hit.

Everyone in attendance at this shindig, whether they're dancing on the small dance floor, swimming in the pool, or sprawled out at tables or in loungers, is visibly having a great time. Even the various dogs running around with Daisy seem to be in doggie heaven.

I'm presently standing next to Selena, chatting with several of the coders on my team. Selena is wearing a blue sundress that flatters her curves. I'm wearing green swim trunks and a "Mariners" baseball cap, with one hand holding Selena's and the other holding my third "Grey Goose Grayson." I'm feeling buzzed and happy, thanks to the booze and pure joy coursing through my bloodstream. I can't believe Selena even thought to throw me a birthday party, let alone such an elaborate, kickass one as this.

Selena hatched the idea about a month ago, during one of our regular family dinners. Selena asked her son what he'd like to do for his fifteenth birthday, which at the time was upcoming in a few months. Specifically, she asked if Drew wanted a big party or, instead, to enjoy some exciting activity with Eddie.

"Which idea sounds more fun to you?" Drew asked me.

"Oh, I'm not the right person to ask," I replied. "Since I've never had a birthday party, I have no basis of comparison."

Drew was flabbergasted. "You've *never* had a birthday party? Not even as a little kid?"

I shook my head. "It's not like my mother ignored my birthday, if that's what you're picturing. She always made my favorite meal for my big day, and I got to have a friend over for a sleepover. My mom and I didn't have family beyond each other, and I wasn't the kind of kid who had tons of friends, so it never occurred to me to ask for a birthday party. Who would I invite?"

Drew asked several more questions about my supposedly unthinkable plight, which I answered with amusement, until, finally, Selena put down her fork with purpose and declared, "Grayson McKnight, I'm going to throw your first-ever birthday party next month."

And now, here we are—and my birthday party is more elaborate than my college buddy's wedding reception. To think *I'm* the guest of honor at this soiree—and that everyone actually knew that's what I'd be when they RSVP'd—is absolutely bananas to me.

I tune back into the conversation around me and surmise that one of my coders, Devlin, is planning a trip to Costa Rica with his husband and that Selena is giving him pointers about where to go and what to see.

"Rent a car and visit at least a couple of their national parks,"

Selena advises. "Also, I'd suggest splitting your time between the beach and the rain forest."

"Oh, let me write this down," our friend says, pulling out his phone. "Thank goodness I happened to bring this up. You're amazing, Selena."

As Devlin begins furiously taking notes, Selena squeezes my arm. "This conversation is reminding me how much I've been wanting to take you to my favorite spots in Costa Rica. Let's look at our calendars tonight and put something on the calendar, okay?"

"Absolutely."

Devlin asks a question, which Selena answers. I listen to the conversation for a bit. But after a while, I can't resist scanning the party, yet again. Truly, I'm blown away this whole thing is for *me*. First off, I spot Drew in the swimming pool and smile at the sight of him. He's playing chicken with Eddie and a couple girls—the same two Selena and I met when we unexpectedly walked in on Drew's movie night months ago. Except these days, the girl on Drew's shoulders is officially his girlfriend.

A couple months after I'd first met Drew, I came over to play video games with him one day, and that's when he asked me for advice on getting the girl who's now sitting on his shoulders to like him "as more than a friend."

"I'm flattered you're asking me," I told Drew back then. "But you should know I've gotten a grand total of two girls to like me as more than a friend in my entire life. One, my college girlfriend. And two, your mom. So, I'm obviously not an expert."

Drew scoffed. "Quality is more important than quantity. That's what Mom always says. So I think, based on the quality of your relationship with my mother, you're an expert on this."

It was a fucking amazing compliment, on so many levels. Indeed, I remember feeling like my heart was going to physically explode with joy in that moment. And yet, somehow, I managed to calmly ask, "What did your dad tell you to do, when you asked him for advice about this?"

I knew I was being a competitive dick to ask the question, but I couldn't resist. I wanted to hear Drew say that whatever advice he'd gotten from Andre didn't ring true, so he decided to come to me next. But to my surprise, Drew revealed he hadn't even talked to his father about the topic at hand and didn't plan to.

"I've seen my father with lots of girlfriends," Drew explained. "And I've seen you with Mom. It's painfully obvious which of you I should ask about women."

That response thrilled me, to put it mildly. I gave Drew whatever advice I could muster, all of it pretty basic stuff. *Ask lots of questions and listen carefully. Remember what she said and bring it up later. Always be yourself.* And not long after that conversation, Drew came to me and excitedly revealed the girl who's now sitting on his shoulders had said yes to their first date. "We're not going out as friends," Drew assured me. "I made it clear this is going to be a real date."

From Drew in the swimming pool, my eyes drift again and land squarely on Max this time. I played corn hole with him earlier today, but he's now sitting at a shaded table with several of Selena's friends, including Marnie, the friend Max hooked up with way back when. I watch Max and Marnie's body language at the table and try to discern if they're flirting over there, but they're too far away for me to come to a conclusion.

Before I look away, Max happens to get up and stride toward the bar, so I excuse myself from my group and head that way, too.

"Hey, Max," I say as we both reach the bar.

He holds up his empty glass. "What the fuck is in this thing besides Grey Goose? It's dangerous."

The bartender pipes in to answer Max's question, and we both order another round. As we wait for our drinks to be made,

I ask, "Any sparks between you and Marnie over there? I saw you sitting with her and her friends."

He shakes his head. "No sparks. At least, not on her end."

I palm my forehead. "Oh, shit. Did you ghost her after you two hooked up, and she's still pissed about it after all this time?"

Before Max answers, the bartender says, "Drinks, fellas."

We grab our cups and move a few feet away to continue our conversation.

"I didn't ghost Marnie," Max says on an exhale. "We never even got each other's numbers or last names."

"Oh. So, why is she pissed? Do you think she's upset at you for not even wanting her number?"

Max puffs out his cheeks. "No, that's not it. She's not pissed at me. Everything's fine."

"But you said there's no spark on *her* end."

He pauses. And then, "I lied to you, Gray. When I said I wasn't interested in seeing her again. The truth is, she blew my mind, and I totally wanted to see her again. In fact, the next morning, I asked her out to dinner, and she said something like, 'This has been a lot of fun, but let's not ruin what's going to be an amazing memory by pretending there's any real potential here.'"

"Holy shit."

"Yeah, I was shocked," Max admits. "I mean, okay, no dinner. Fine. But at the very least, didn't she want to hook up with me again? The sex was fire! Off-the-charts for both of us. Plus, I'm positive she didn't wake up and realize she'd been wearing beer goggles, because when we woke up the next morning, she practically attacked me. And the sex was fire again, even when we were both completely sober."

"Wow."

Max runs his hand through his hair. Clearly, the dude's at a loss. "After we had sex in the morning, we started talking about where we should go for breakfast . . . So, I know she was feeling it. Why else would she talk about having breakfast with me?" He shakes his head. "I went into the bathroom to do my thing, while Marnie stayed in bed looking at nearby breakfast places on her phone. And by the time I came out, she was dressed and clearly heading out the door. If I hadn't come out when I did, I'm positive she would have been gone."

"Without even saying goodbye?"

Nodding, Max looks over at Marnie's table, where the women are chatting and drinking. "I asked her what's wrong and she said something came up. I said no problem, let's do dinner tonight. And that's when she said that thing about not ruining a memory."

"Oof. Brutal."

"What am I missing? Is she married? While I was in the bathroom, did her husband text that he was home early from a work trip?"

"That can't be it. Marnie's been single as long as I've known her. She's always got funny stories about her dating life."

Max murmurs, "What, then? What the fuck changed?"

I twist my mouth. "Did she maybe have access to your phone while you were in the bathroom? God knows what she might have seen on it, Max."

Max shakes his head. "I had my phone in the bathroom with me. I'm not an idiot."

"Is today the first time you're seeing her since that morning?"

He nods.

"Okay, so pull her aside and ask her what the fuck happened. If it were me, I'd go crazy if I didn't get some kind of closure."

Max gazes at Marnie's table for a long moment, before shaking his head and saying, "Nah. When I first sat down at her table, I was kind of hoping she'd flirt with me. Maybe even make it clear she's down for another hookup. But nope. She barely looked at me, even when her friends were talking directly to me. So, fuck it. There's no point in asking her about it. I'm not going to give her the satisfaction. If she's not feeling it with me, fine. It's her loss."

Max's face doesn't match his words, I notice. No matter what he's saying, it's clear to me Max thinks this situation with Marnie has been *his* loss.

"I'm sorry, Max. That's a bummer."

He shrugs. "Such is life. I mean, it's not usually *my* life, but I guess there's a first for everything." He says something else, but I'm abruptly too distracted by a figure walking into the party to hear it.

"Motherfucker," I mutter through clenched teeth. "*Andre.* He's crashing my birthday party." Indeed, the asshole is striding into the back yard like he's got an engraved invitation in his pocket. And worst of all, he's heading straight for Selena.

21

GRAYSON

Max follows my gaze to Andre, who's quickly closing the gap between him and Selena. Clearly, she's his destination.

"Don't let him spot me," Max mutters, stepping behind my back. "I'm supposed to be prepping one of Andre's cases today."

My jaw muscles pulse. "He's not here to crack the whip on a lowly associate, Max. He's here to ruin my girlfriend's good time." Shit. If ever there was a time when the word "girlfriend" felt wholly insufficient, now is that time.

With my heart crashing, I watch Andre reach Selena and tap her on the shoulder. I don't know why my hackles have instantly gone up at the sight of him. I hate that man with the force of a thousand suns, yes, but I'm well aware he's Drew's father, whether I like it or not, so it's logical to think he might reasonably have something to say to his kid's mother.

But today of all days?

After touching Selena's shoulder, Andre says something to her that causes her visible consternation. She motions vaguely to the party surrounding them, as if to say, "Now isn't a good time,

Andre." But a moment later, she follows him away from the party, stiffly, with both of them walking toward the house.

"Motherfucker!" I grit out. I hand Max my drink. "Hold this for me, in case I need to throw down."

"If you need back-up, I can't help you," Max shouts toward my retreating back. "Sorry, but he's my boss!"

"I won't need backup," I spit out over my shoulder.

Surely, whatever's brought Andre to my birthday party won't lead to physical violence, unfortunately, despite my ardent hope that Andre will finally provoke me beyond the limits of my self-control. Since my first encounter with that bastard in that restaurant so long ago, I've secretly fantasized, countless times, about one day finally getting to break his perfectly tanned face. In fact, in addition to me wanting to look as good as possible for Selena, the fantasy of me getting strong enough to take Andre down has been a major motivator to get my ass into the gym, consistently. But, still, I've crossed paths with Andre several times, briefly, mostly at Drew's various school events, and we've both always managed to keep our mutual hatred from boiling over into an altercation for Drew's sake.

I reach the far end of the patio where Selena and Andre disappeared around the corner of the house a moment ago and stop short when I hear Selena's angry voice.

"You've got to be fucking kidding me," Selena is saying.

I peek around the corner like a creeper, my blood simmering and my skin tingling, and discover Selena and Andre standing about twenty yards away in a small patio area. They're facing each other, such that they're both in profile to me, and Selena's body language makes it clear she's deadass enraged at Andre.

"Look, I know I blew it with you, but—"

"The understatement of the century!" Selena bellows, looking absolutely livid.

"But that was then. I'm here *now* to ask you—to *beg* you—to give me a second chance. And you know I don't beg."

What the fuck did that fucker say to my woman? I take a step forward, intent on hurling myself at Andre and tackling him. But Selena's voice stops me.

"How dare you come to my house and say this crazy shit to me," she yells. "Especially on the day of my beloved boyfriend's birthday party! That's so disrespectful!"

You tell him, baby. Good one.

Andre scoffs. "I had no idea you were throwing the kid a birthday party. Drew left some shoes at my place, so I decided to bring them over and use the opportunity to tell you what I've been thinking about for months now. I know I've made mistakes, Selena."

"No shit."

"I know I had some things to sort out. Lessons to learn. But I've learned those lessons, and I'm a new man now. I think we both owe it to Drew, to ourselves, to our *family*, to give our marriage a second chance."

Asshole.

I physically clutch the edge of the house, keeping myself from running over there and knocking Andre's teeth out of his mouth. Something tells me Selena wouldn't appreciate me inserting myself into this private conversation. At least, not yet. Thus far, she's certainly been handing Andre his ass without any assistance from me.

"Divorcing you was the best thing I ever did for myself and Drew," Selena says evenly. "There's not a single molecule in my body that wants you back. I'm in love with someone else now, but I wouldn't take you back, even if I were single. I'd rather be alone than with you, Andre."

Boom. That's right, baby. Give him hell.

Andre says, "That's ridiculous, Selena. Come on. You know I can take care of you, better than anyone else. And for my part, I've realized there's never going to be anyone who understands me the way you always have. I took that for granted when we were married. I thought the grass would be greener somewhere else. But now I realize that—"

"First of all, I don't 'understand' you and never did, you fucking narcissist," Selena says. "*I was scared of you.* I said and did all the right things to never piss you off. Keeping you happy and feeding your ego, ensuring you'd never become angry, became my goddamned survival skill!"

I can practically hear Andre's eyeroll from here. "Always so dramatic. I never laid a hand on you, and you know it."

"You punched walls! You screamed at me and got into my face. You threw me in that closet and locked the door!"

"That was only once, and I was drunk."

"Yeah, and I was terrified. After that, I always knew, if I said or did the wrong thing, you might lose your temper and do God knows what to me."

"You knew I'd never actually hurt you."

"I did *not* know that! So, as far as you 'taking care of me,' that's literally the opposite of what you did to me. You terrified me, Andre. I lived in constant fear!"

"Stop being so dramatic. Do you think it's easy for me to come here and admit I fucked up? But here I am, with my proverbial hat in my hands, admitting that I was wrong. The least you can do is give me the courtesy of seriously considering what I have to say."

"I owe you nothing. Don't you realize what you're feeling isn't love? It's jealousy! I'm sure Drew tells you all the time how deliriously happy I am with Grayson, and it enrages you to no end to know I've found someone who loves me like you never could. I'm sure Drew even told you about today's birthday party, didn't he? So, you came over here to make a scene, to try to ruin Grayson's happy day, not because you want *me*, not because you *ever* wanted me, but because you can't stand to lose. Because if you can't have me, then you don't want any other man to have me, either."

"Damn straight, I don't! Especially not some little boy who looks like a fucking paid escort on your arm!"

"*What?*"

"Everyone can see he's a loser who doesn't have two nickels to rub together! I swear to God, I'm sick to death of our son having to witness his mother making a goddamned fool of herself by flaunting her relationship with a nobody. Where's your self-respect, Selena? *Set a good example for our son.*"

"Okay, that's it," Selena barks. "Get the fuck out—right fucking now—or I'll call the police!"

And that's my cue. I burst around the corner of the house, sprint toward Andre, and push on his chest. "The lady told you to get the fuck out," I yell, as Andre stumbles back in shock. "Time to go, asshole."

"Grayson," Selena gasps behind me. She sounds equal parts relieved and alarmed.

When Andre gets his feet steady underneath him, he strikes a laughable power pose across from me. Chest puffed. Chin up. Arms flexed. If we were two silverbacks, Andre would be beating his chest. "This doesn't concern you, little boy," he seethes. "This is between me and my wife."

"*Ex*-wife," I shout, as Selena says the same thing behind me.

"Everyone can see you're a *gold digger*," Andre shouts at me. "Must be nice to get to hang out at your rich girlfriend's house all the time, huh? Save yourself big bucks on rent and food?"

I lunge forward and shove my face into Andre's, physically quaking with the urge to pummel his face. "I'm warning you, old man. Shut your fucking mouth before I break it."

Andre smiles. "Do it, gold digger. Show me what you've got." He touches his chin. "Right here. Hit me as hard as you can, little boy. I bet the only thing you'll break is your hand."

Trembling, I clench my fist. There's nothing I want more than to beat the living shit out of this man. He deserves it for all the times he mistreated Selena. For the shitty example he sets for Drew. And for all the years he undeservedly held the title of "Selena's husband." I'm not a violent guy by nature, but this asshole evokes a murderous streak in me I didn't know I had. Looking into his dark eyes and seeing that taunting, arrogant look in them, I want nothing more than to unleash all my rage onto his face.

"Don't do it, Grayson!" Selena shouts behind me. She clutches my flexed bicep. "He's baiting you!"

"Aw, come on, little boy. Wouldn't it feel good to punch me? *I dare you.*"

I'm quaking. Tingling. But I take a deep breath and take a step back, suddenly realizing Selena is exactly right. This motherfucker is baiting me. Setting some kind of trap.

Andre is a renowned lawyer, after all—one of Seattle's best. If I beat the shit out of him now, as he's explicitly daring me to do, he'd surely turn around and gleefully sue me for everything I've got, including all my shares in my new company. Or maybe his real endgame is finding a way to keep me away from his son by turning me into a supposedly violent lunatic? That'd be a clever back-door way to keep me away from Selena, too, at least whenever Drew is staying with his mother. Fucking hell. Whatever Andre's ultimate goal, it's now clear to me he's willing to sacrifice his face to accomplish it. This is most definitely a trap —one Andre is hoping I'm too young and testosterone-laden to figure out.

"Come on," Andre spits out. "You pussy-ass little golddigger. *Hit me.* Show Selena how big and strong you are. Show her you'll always protect her from the big, bad wolf."

My breathing is shallow, and my cheeks are on fire. I choke out, "I want nothing more than to break your face, for all the times you scared, hurt, or betrayed Selena. But I'm not going to let you bait me into fucking up my entire life. Not only for myself and Selena, but for Drew. If I beat the shit out of his father, he'd feel like he has to pick sides between us—like he couldn't even invite both his father and *stepfather* to his future high school graduation."

At my use of the word *stepfather*, Andre's dark eyes ignite, and I know my arrow has hit its intended bull's-eye.

"I'd never hurt Drew like that," I say, "no matter how amazing it'd feel to break your jaw. Fuck that. *And fuck you*." With that, I grab Selena's hand and march with her toward the corner of the house. But before turning the corner, I stop short, causing Selena to stop with me. I pivot toward Andre. "I know you think you're insulting *me* by calling me a gold-digger," I say. "But you're actually insulting Selena. The fact that you think I could only want to be with her for her money, and not because she's the most amazing woman in the world, sums up everything that's wrong with you. Not that it's any of your business, but I love this woman for her beautiful heart and soul. I love her because she makes me happier than I thought possible. Because I admire her. Because she's a great mom. Because she's funny and kind. I physically ache when I'm away from her. I love this woman for *her* and always will—for richer or poorer, in sickness or health, till death do us part—so you'd better get fucking used to having me around." I flip him off. "Now, get the fuck off my future wife's property, or I'll call the police and report you for trespassing."

"Grayson would be well within his rights to make that phone call," Selena adds. "Since this is his home, too."

That's news to me. But, of course, I nod energetically and say, "That's right."

"Oh, and Andre?" Selena says. "Not that it's any of your business, but this little boy's dick is at least twice the size of yours—and I gleefully let him do *anything* he wants with it, including letting him put it *anywhere*." As I make a sound best described as a snorfle, Selena grips my hand and says, "Come on, Big Boy. Life is short, and this man has already wasted far too much of my valuable time."

22

SELENA

"You were amazing back there!" Grayson gushes enthusiastically.

We're inside my house now—in my home office with the door closed. I figured nobody from the party would wander into this particular room, so I dragged Grayson in here to talk about the batshit crazy thing that just went down with Andre.

"You handled him perfectly," Grayson adds. "I was so proud of your badassery!"

"I'm sorry if I embarrassed you by mentioning your dick," I say. "That's none of Andre's business."

"Are you kidding?" Grayson says. "Ha! That was the best part! That, and how you implied you let me fuck you up the ass." Grayson hoots with laughter. "Oh my God! Did you see his face?"

I cringe. "Do you think Andre knew that's what I meant? I wanted him to know we do that, since he used to beg for it, constantly, to no avail, but I didn't want to say 'anal sex' explicitly."

Grayson looks thoroughly amused. "Trust me, your message was received, loud and clear."

I palm my forehead. "Oh my God. I'm still shaking. I can't believe the crazy stuff he said." Grayson wraps his strong arms around me, and I lay my cheek on his chest, murmuring, "I'm so glad you showed up when you did. He's so scary."

Grayson kisses the top of my head. "I was watching you the whole time, baby. I didn't want to get in your way while you were kicking ass, but I had your back."

"You showed up at the perfect time. You were Superman."

"I bet it felt amazing to tell him off."

"It did. But I was thrilled when you showed up. I was shaking so hard."

He kisses my temple. "I'm sorry if I screwed up by calling you my future wife or by saying I'm going to be Drew's stepfather one day. I'm sure both things will get back to Drew."

"I'm not sorry you said either thing. In fact, I'm glad you did. You made me swoon so hard."

Grayson pulls back from our embrace and looks into my eyes. "Really?"

"Oh, God, yes." As we share a smile, I telepathically scream at him, *Ask me now, Grayson! Ask me and I'll say yes!* But he doesn't do it. Instead, he pecks me on the cheek and strides to the window, murmuring something about making sure Andre is gone.

At the window, Grayson parts the blinds with two fingers and peeks out at the back yard. "I don't see him anywhere in the party," he reports. "I should probably check out front to make sure his car is gone."

I take a deep breath. I'm feeling the impulse to walk over to Grayson, take his face in my hands, and propose to him myself. I'm a modern woman, after all. And I know he'd say yes to me.

But no.

Despite what my heart wants to do, my brain knows this probably isn't the right time, what with Andre potentially lurking around and Grayson still looking so amped up and distracted. Not to mention, after all the times Grayson has casually proposed to me—in bed, in the hot tub, in the shower—I think he deserves to finally hear me say "yes" in reply to a more traditional, formal proposal. The more I think about it, I wouldn't want to steal his thunder.

"Yeah, I think that's a good idea," I say, referring to Grayson heading to the front of the house. "But, honey, if Andre is out there, *please* be careful. If you lay a pinky on that man, he'll sue you for assault and try to destroy you."

"No worries, love. I know exactly what game he's playing. If he strikes first, he's going down. But otherwise, I promise to keep my cool." He kisses my cheek. "Go back to the party. I'll be right behind you, once I'm sure he's gone."

Back in the party, I find my friends and tell them everything that happened with Andre and Grayson, and they practically explode with comments, questions, and exclamations.

"Where is Grayson?" Victoria asks after a while, looking around.

"He's making sure Andre left," I explain. But I've no sooner said the words than my phone buzzes with an incoming text from the birthday boy himself.

> Grayson: No sign of A or his car out front. Talked to Mr. Peterson. He's been outside mowing his front lawn for the past twenty minutes. He confirmed A drove away.

> Me: Huzzah. Come back to the party, birthday boy. We'll bring out the birthday cake and champagne!

> Grayson: Need a quick bathroom break. Be there in five.

I reply with thumbs-up and heart emojis and resume chatting with my girlfriends. But a few minutes later, my phone buzzes with yet another text from Grayson.

> Grayson: Hey, Hot Teacher. I'm hoping you've got time to give me some much-needed advice.

> Me: Hey there, Grayson-hopper! I've always got time for you. What's up?

> Grayson: I have this amazing girlfriend I'm so in love with, it hurts, and I'm planning to ask her to marry me. Something big just happened that's thrown me for a loop, and now I need some guidance on how to pop the question to her.

> Me: You're getting married? How exciting! Congratulations!

> Grayson: Assuming she says yes.

> Me: Oh, she will. Your girlfriend would have to be a damned fool to turn you down. Is she a damned fool?

> Grayson: LOL. No, she's the smartest person I know.

> Me: Then she'll say yes. I'm sure of it.

> Grayson: Thank God. Okay, so here's the thing. I've already got a romantic proposal with all the bells and whistles planned in a couple weeks. But after a near-altercation with her ex a few minutes ago, I suddenly feel like I can't wait another minute to call her my fiancée and future wife. So now, I'm thinking of scrapping my original plan and doing it now.

> Me: DO IT.

> Grayson: You think? The thing is we're at my birthday party with tons of our friends and family, and my girlfriend once made a comment about not being a fan of public proposals.

Oh, hell. I knew I'd unwittingly messed with Grayson's head when I said that thing at the basketball game, right after we witnessed a stranger proposing at center court. It was written all over Grayson's face that he was thinking, "Note to self. *No public proposals.*"

> Me: Honey, this wouldn't be a public proposal. It's your birthday party with family and friends! I'm sure your girlfriend will be thrilled to share this special day with them, especially after watching you spring to action like a superhero with her horrible ex. As a matter of fact, a little birdie told me she thought you were insanely sexy and swoony when you did that.

> Grayson: Hehe. Not gonna lie. It was hot.

> Me: I bet it was. Honestly, I can't think of a better time to ask her than RIGHT FUCKING NOW.

> Grayson: Holy shit! Okay. I'd better go now. My girlfriend thinks I'm taking a bathroom break and I wouldn't want her getting suspicious that I'm up to something.

> Me: Good idea. Wouldn't want to ruin the surprise.

> Grayson: Exactly. Thanks, Hot Teacher. You're the best.

> Me: Any time, Grayson-hopper. It's always a pleasure. I'd wish you good luck with your proposal, but I'm confident you don't need it.

I send Grayson a heart emoji, and the next thing I know, he's striding out of the back door of the house, across the patio, and straight toward me. When he reaches me, he wordlessly takes me into his arms and kisses me passionately, which causes everyone around us to cheer and clap.

"Whoa," I whisper when he releases my lips. "That was quite a kiss."

"Come with me," he commands. Without explaining himself, he takes my hand and leads me to the DJ booth, where he asks the guy to turn off the music and hand him a mic.

"Hey, everyone," Grayson says to the party, as I stand next to him, trembling with anticipation. "Thanks so much for coming today."

The crowd shouts, "Happy birthday, Grayson!" and "We love you, Grayson!"

"I want to thank Selena for throwing me this shindig. It's my first-ever birthday party, and the ten-year-old inside me has been shouting 'This is so sick!' all day long."

As everyone laughs, I look for Drew in the crowd to make sure he's here to witness whatever is about to happen, and I'm thrilled to see my son is now out of the pool and standing nearby, his face awash with pure joy. I look at my father and catch his eye, and his smile is wide and beaming. I glance at Grayson's mother, and she also looks absolutely delighted.

"Selena," Grayson says, prompting me to return my gaze to him. "There's something I want to ask you." His Adam's apple bobs. "Something I've been dreaming about asking you, since the first moment I saw you—because that's when I first fell head over heels in love with you."

The crowd titters lightly with anticipation.

"You make me happier than I knew was possible," Grayson says. "I love you so much."

"I love you, too," I manage to say, even though there's a lump in my throat.

Without further ado, Grayson sinks to his knee before me and, to my shock, holds up a closed ring box. Why didn't I expect this diehard romantic to get me a ring? I should have known.

As the crowd gasps at the obvious implications of Grayson's posture, he looks up at me with teary eyes and says, "My love. My life. My pulchritudinous goddess. Selena Diaz, will you make me the happiest man in the world and marry me?"

"Yes!" I shout enthusiastically, at which point Grayson opens the lid of the box to reveal a dazzling, princess-cut diamond ring inside. It's a sparkler that so damned stunning, it causes me to scream. "Grayson McKnight!" I shriek. "What have you done?"

As the crowd cheers and applauds, Grayson rises, slides the ring on my finger, and pulls me into a kiss. After releasing my lips, Grayson nuzzles my nose and whispers, "Happy birthday to me."

"The ring, Grayson," I blurt, my head spinning. "It's too much. Too expensive."

"Do you like it?"

"I love it. I love you. But it's too much."

"I can afford it, just fine," he assures me. "All that matters is that you love it and you'll be proud to wear it."

"So proud," I choke out through my brimming emotion. "I love you. Oh my God."

We're suddenly surrounded by all the people we love most in the world. Even Daisy has joined the congratulatory swarm, offering a wagging tail and lots of kisses.

As Grayson and I accept hugs, kisses, and congratulations, the caterer wheels out the cake and starts passing around champagne for a toast. When everyone has a glass of some sort, Grayson brings the microphone to his lips again.

"Before we cut the cake," he says, "I want to thank a few important people. First off, to my mom. Thanks for making the trip down here today and for welcoming Selena into our family." We blow Grayson's mother kisses and take sips in her honor, and she looks tickled pink. Next up, Grayson finds my father in the crowd and raises his glass again. "To Selena's father. Pops. Thank you for welcoming me into your family. I promise I'll always take the best care of your daughter." After the men exchange smiles and waves and I've blown my father a multitude of kisses, we drink to my father, along with the crowd. Next, Grayson finds Drew's smiling face. "Drew. I love you, kid. You're wise beyond your years. Funny as hell. And a damned amazing Dungeon Master." When the crowd titters, Grayson adds, "That's a reference to a game called Dungeons & Dragons. Not BDSM."

Everyone howls with laughter, including me.

"Oh, Grayson," I murmur, feeling myself blush.

"*Anyway*," Grayson says, returning his gaze to Drew. "I sadly missed your first word. Your first step. But I'm not going to miss out on anything else, from this day forward. To Drew!"

After the crowd joins Grayson and me in raising their glasses to Drew, I take the microphone. "Drew was actually the one who made me see that the age gap between Grayson and me didn't matter," I say. "He told me to live my life and love out in the open without apology. And he was right. That's the only way to live. Thank you, Drew. You've been warm and welcoming to Grayson from day one and a true blessing to me since the day you were born. I love you so much."

Drew shoots me finger-guns, making me chuckle, and then salutes Grayson.

I bring the mic to my lips again. "There's one last 'very important person' Grayson and I need to thank, before we get back to our regularly scheduled programming and let the birthday boy blow out his candles. Actually, this person, more than anyone else, is responsible for Grayson and me getting together." I shoot a wicked grin at Grayson. "*Katie*. Thank you, girl, wherever you are. We owe you one."

Of course, Grayson bursts out laughing at my inside joke, but everyone else at the party looks visibly confused.

As much as I'm enjoying the looks of befuddlement all around me, I decide to let the crowd in on our joke. "Katie is the fool who gave Grayson a fake number in a bar about a year and a half ago," I explain to the crowd. "And unwittingly led him straight to me, his future wife." I smile at Grayson again. "His *fate*."

"Amen," Grayson whispers. He kisses my cheek and then raises his glass. "To Katie!"

The party enthusiastically echoes Grayson's toast, and then mine, as well, when I shout, "To fate!"

As everyone around me drinks, I throw my champagne back with gusto, feeling euphoric. With my bubbly gone, I slide my arms around my new fiancé's neck and laugh with glee. I can't believe that wrong-number text brought us here—and I wouldn't have it any other way.

"I love you so much," I say to Grayson. "That was a perfect

proposal, honey. I absolutely loved it. The perfect proposal for a perfect day."

Grayson nuzzles my nose. "I promise this is only the beginning for us, my love—the first of endless perfect days of our happily ever after."

EPILOGUE
SELENA

"Daisy, here!" I call out. But the damned dog is too excited in her reindeer antlers and jingle bells to stay put for our family photo in front of the Christmas tree. In fact, our old girl is surprisingly spry as she bounds around our family room like a runaway reindeer, leaving the rest of the family—myself, Grayson, Drew, and our three-year-old, Olivia, the blessing we adopted fourteen months ago—posed and waiting in front of Grayson's tripod.

"Daisy-girl, come here," Grayson coos calmly, his tone like warm honey. And, of course, the dog obeys her all-time favorite person, the same way she always does. I swear, as much as my beloved fur baby has always adored Drew and me, when she first laid eyes on Grayson seven years ago, she decided the tall man with the gentle spirit and calming voice was *hers*. Can't say I blame the dog, given that I had pretty much the same reaction to Grayson the first time I saw him, too. When Grayson flashed me that wide, mega-watt smile at Captain's all those years ago, I think I knew right then, somewhere in my soul, I was already a goner.

"That's my good girl," Grayson coos to Daisy, scratching the top of her head. But then, he goes on to say something that makes me press my lips together with impatience: "You want Daisy to stand next to you this time, Livvy?" Obviously, Olivia will answer her daddy's question affirmatively, and I think it's fifty-fifty re-positioning Daisy, especially on the far end of our family photo from Grayson, will throw our photo session into barely contained chaos, yet again.

Not surprisingly, Olivia responds enthusiastically, clapping her little hands and shouting "Daisyyyyy!" So, Drew, who's best positioned to finesse this new configuration, takes the initiative without being asked, quickly grabbing Daisy by her collar and gently guiding her into position at Olivia's little feet.

With the dog now sitting next to her, Olivia squeals and does a happy little shimmy that's so adorable, my heart feels like it's exploding at the sight of her . . . which only makes me chastise myself for momentarily forgetting what Grayson always says about times like these: *It's the journey, not the destination, babe.*

It's no wonder that's one of Grayson's favorite expressions, because it's the perfect one to describe our life together, especially since we adopted Olivia. With Grayson as my husband, best friend, and teammate, life truly has been a most beautiful journey—or, rather, a most "pulchritudinous" one, as Grayson is so fond of saying.

Through Grayson's example, from watching him steadfastly demonstrate unwavering love for me and our family, I've learned to savor even the simplest of interactions with him, and also with Olivia and Drew, as well, whenever Drew is home from school. Grayson has taught me to stop thinking ahead so much, to stop planning and trying to control what happens in life, but instead to be present in the moment and enjoy whatever comes our way, including unexpected curveballs.

"Okay, let's try this again," Grayson says brightly, loping toward the camera on his tripod. "I'll set the timer for only five seconds this time. Hold onto Daisy's collar, Livvy Loo!"

"I am!" Olivia shouts excitedly.

"That's my girl!" Grayson looks through the viewfinder of his fancy camera. "Squish a little closer to Mommy, Livvy Loo!"

"Like dis?"

"Perfect! Okay, here we go!" After pushing the button on the timer, my husband bounds back to his spot between Olivia and me, slides an arm around my shoulders, places his free hand on our daughter's tiny shoulder, and shouts, "Say 'cheese and macamomi,' everyone!"

"Cheese and macamomi!" we all bellow happily, mimicking the way Olivia always says it, and when Olivia's high-pitched squeak of a voice gleefully cuts through the rest, Drew, Grayson, and I can't help giggling, precisely as the camera snaps its shot.

"Woohoo!" Grayson says. "I think we got a good one that time!"

As I pick up Olivia and rest her on my hip, Grayson heads to the camera to see if we've managed to finally capture gold.

"We did it!" he announces.

"Is it pokey-toody, Daddy?" Olivia says, trying to enunciate her father's all-time favorite word—which, not surprisingly, he calls Olivia every night at bedtime—and, of course, we all chuckle at her adorable mispronunciation.

"It sure is, honey bear," Grayson says, thankfully not correcting her. Grayson and I have talked about it and agreed that Olivia will learn how to say pulchritudinous, soon enough, as well as "gloves" instead of "glubbs," and "earth" instead of "erff," even without us correcting her now. So why deprive ourselves of these adorable, fleeting moments with Olivia that will surely turn into nothing but precious memories on their own, soon enough?

"Hey, Mom," Drew says, and I peel my eyes off Grayson and Olivia, who are now playing pony on the family room floor. "I'm gonna go pick up Cassie at the airport." He's talking about his girlfriend, a young woman who runs track at their university and aspires to become a pediatrician one day. Drew continues, "Do you want me to pick up some pizzas for dinner on the way back?"

I shake my head. "I made a couple lasagnas last night. All I have to do is pop them into the oven. I'll do that now, so they'll be ready when you get back."

"Bless you, woman." He kisses my cheek. "God, I've missed your home-cooking."

Olivia squeals, drawing our attention, and we both chuckle at the way Grayson is neighing with Olivia on his back.

"Will you make Cassie a cake when she gets here, Livvy?" Drew asks. He's referring to the plastic cooking set he sent Olivia for her third birthday last month.

Olivia replies in the affirmative, but a second later, she's too distracted by her neighing daddy to pay her big brother any further mind.

Smiling, Drew returns to me. "I'd better get going. I want to be at the airport early, so I can park and meet Cassie at baggage claim, rather than at the curb."

"Good boy."

It's a classic Grayson move—being early for an airport pick-up—or any pick-up or event, really—that man is never late for anything. And that only serves to remind me, once again, what a tremendously positive influence my darling husband has been on my son.

When Drew leaves, I crawl onto the ground and join Grayson and Olivia's game for a bit. I think the three of us are lions. If not, nobody is correcting me.

"*Rawr*," Grayson whispers, shoving his face into mine. "That's big-cat for, 'I love you.'"

I rub my nose against Grayson's. "*Rawr* to you, too. So, so much." I peck his lips and then turn to Olivia to boop her little nose. "And *rawr* to you, too, my little cub."

"Rawrrrrr!" Olivia replies heartily, baring her tiny teeth and scrunching her nose.

I laugh. "Wow, that's a big roar! Are you hungry, my little lion?"

"I'm a tiger, Mommy."

"Wonderful. Are you hungry, my little tiger cub? Yes? Me, too."

Grayson looks around the family room. "Did Drew already leave to get Cassie?"

"He just left. I'd better put the lasagnas in the oven, so they'll be ready when they get back." I get up off the floor and head toward the kitchen with Daisy the Dog following me. But I can't resist turning around in the doorway for one last look at Grayson and Olivia on the floor.

I never dreamed my life could turn out like this, back when Grayson sent me that wrong-number text all those years ago. Not in my wildest dreams. But now that I'm here, I know that's because this life with Grayson—my husband, my lover, my best friend, my *destiny*—is better than I was even capable of dreaming about, even in my wildest of wild dreams. Grayson once promised me a happily ever after. And that's exactly what that sweet man has given me.

THE END

Want to know what happened behind the scenes with Max and Marnie? It's a spicy, funny, shocking doozy of a love story! Check out *Who's Your Daddy: An older woman/younger man rom com*.

Remember the hunky, tattooed bartender with ocean eyes at Captain's—the one who served Selena that martini the night she first met Grayson? He's Ryan Morgan, the owner of Captain's, and the origin story of how he met, lost, and then wooed the woman of his dreams—going after her like Captain Ahab on Moby Dick—will make you laugh, swoon, and fan yourself. Check out Captain

Note: *Captain* is listed as number two in the standalone *Morgan Brothers* series of books, but it's a great place to start. In fact, that book is listed as the first standalone book in other languages.

Or, if you prefer, feel free to check out any of the romance titles in Lauren's catalogue, described below. **All books by Lauren Rowe are available in ebook, paperback, and audiobook formats.**

BOOKS BY LAUREN ROWE

STANDALONE Romantic Comedy Series

Who's Your Daddy?

When thirty-year-old patent attorney, Maximillian Vaughn, meets a sassy, charismatic older woman in a bar, he invites her back to his place for one night of no-strings fun. It's all Max can offer, given his busy career; but, luckily, it's all Marnie wants, too. But when Max's chemistry with Marnie is so combustible, it threatens to burn down his bedroom, he does the unthinkable the next morning: he asks Marnie out on a dinner date.

Mere minutes after saying yes, however, Marnie bolts like her hair is on fire with no explanation. What happened? Max doesn't know, but he's determined to find out and convince Marnie to pick up where they left off.

Textual Relations

When Grayson McKnight unknowingly gets a fake number from a woman in a bar, he winds up embroiled in a sexy text exchange with the actual owner of the number—a confident, sensual older woman who knows exactly who she is . . . and what she wants.

No strings attached.

But as sparks fly and real feelings develop, will Grayson get his way and tempt her to give him more than their original bargain?

My Neighbors Secret

When Charlotte gets into her new dilapidated condo to start fixing it up for resale, she finds out the infuriating stranger who's thoroughly messed up her life is her new next-door neighbor.

Also, that he's got a big secret.

She confronts him and proposes they work together to get themselves out of their respective jams, even though they both admittedly can't stand each other. Yes, he's let it slip he thinks she's pretty. And, okay, she begrudgingly thinks he's kind of cute. But whatever. They hate each other and this is nothing but a business partnership. What could go wrong?

The Secret Note

He's a hot Aussie. I'm a girl who isn't shy about getting what she wants. The problem? Ben is my little brother's best friend. An exchange student who's heading back Down Under any day now. But I can't help myself. He's too hot to resist.

Dive into Lauren's universe of interconnected trilogies and duets, all books available individually and as a bundle, in any order.

A full suggested reading order can be found here!

The Josh & Kat Trilogy

It's a war of wills between stubborn and sexy Josh Faraday and Kat Morgan. A fight to the bed. Arrogant, wealthy playboy Josh is used to getting what he wants. And what he wants is Kat Morgan. The books are to be read in order:

Infatuation

Revelation

Consummation

The Club Trilogy

When wealthy playboy Jonas Faraday receives an anonymous note from Sarah Cruz, a law student working part-time processing online applications for an exclusive club, he becomes obsessed with hunting her down and giving her the satisfaction she claims has always eluded her. Thus begins a sweeping tale of obsession, passion, desperation, and ultimately, everlasting love and individual redemption. Find out why scores of readers all over the world, in multiple languages, call The Club Trilogy "my favorite trilogy ever" and "the greatest love story I've ever read." As Jonas Faraday says to Sarah Cruz: "There's never been a love like ours and there never will be again… Our love is so pure and true, we're the amazement of the gods."

The Club: Obsession

The Club: Reclamation

The Club: Redemption

The fourth book for Jonas and Sarah is a full-length epilogue with incredible heart-stopping twists and turns and feels. Read The Club: Culmination (A Full-Length Epilogue Novel) after finishing The Club Trilogy or, if you prefer, after reading The Josh and Kat Trilogy.

The Reed Rivers Trilogy

Reed Rivers has met his match in the most unlikely of women—aspiring journalist and spitfire, Georgina Ricci. She's much younger than the women Reed normally pursues, but he can't resist her fiery personality and drop-dead gorgeous looks. But in this game of cat and mouse, who's chasing whom? With each passing day of this wild ride, Reed's not so sure. The books of this trilogy are to be read in order:

Bad Liar

Beautiful Liar

Beloved Liar

The Hate Love Duet

An addicting, enemies-to-lovers romance with humor, heat, angst, and banter. Music artists Savage of Fugitive Summer and Laila Fitzgerald are stuck together on tour. And convinced they can't stand each other. What they don't know is that they're absolutely made for each other, whether they realize it or not. The books of this duet are to be read in order:

Falling Out of Hate with You

Falling Into Love with You

Interconnected Standalones within the same universe as above

Hacker in Love

When world-class hacker Peter "Henn" Hennessey meets Hannah Milliken, he moves heaven and earth, including doing some questionable things, to win his dream girl over. But when catastrophe strikes, will Henn lose Hannah forever, or is there still a chance for him to chase their happily ever after? *Hacker in Love* is a steamy, funny, heart-pounding, **standalone** contemporary romance with a whole lot of feels, laughs, spice, and swoons.

Smitten

When aspiring singer-songwriter, Alessandra, meets Fish, the funny, adorable bass player of 22 Goats, sparks fly between the awkward pair. Fish tells Alessandra he's a "Goat called Fish who's hung like a bull. But not really. I'm actually really average." And Alessandra tells Fish, "There's nothing like a girl's first love." Alessandra thinks she's talking about a song when she makes her comment to Fish—the first song she'd ever heard by 22 Goats, in fact. As she'll later find out, though, her "first love" was actually Fish. The Goat called Fish who, after that night, vowed to do anything to win her heart. SMITTEN is a true standalone romance.

Swoon

When Colin Beretta, the drummer of 22 Goats, is a groomsman at the wedding of his childhood best friend, Logan, he discovers Logan's kid sister, Amy, is all grown up. Colin tries to resist his attraction to Amy, but after a drunken kiss at the wedding reception, that's easier said than done. Swoon is a true standalone romance.

The Morgan Brothers

Read these standalones in any order about the brothers of Kat Morgan. Chronological reading order is below, but they are all complete stories. Note: you do not need to read any other books or series before jumping straight into reading about the Morgan boys.

Hero

The story of heroic firefighter, Colby Morgan. When catastrophe strikes Colby Morgan, will physical therapist Lydia save him . . . or will he save her?

Captain

The insta-love-to-enemies-to-lovers story of tattooed sex god, Ryan Morgan, and the woman he'd move heaven and earth to claim.

Ball Peen Hammer

A steamy, hilarious, friends-to-lovers romantic comedy about cocky-as-hell male stripper, Keane Morgan, and the sassy, smart young woman who brings him to his knees during a road trip.

Mister Bodyguard

The Morgans' beloved honorary brother, Zander Shaw, meets his match in the feisty pop star he's assigned to protect on tour.

ROCKSTAR

When the youngest Morgan brother, Dax Morgan, meets a mysterious woman who rocks his world, he must decide if pursuing her is worth risking it all. Be sure to check out four of Dax's original songs from ROCKSTAR, written and produced by Lauren, along with full music videos for the songs, on her website (www.laurenrowebooks.com) under the tab MUSIC FROM ROCKSTAR.

Misadventures Standalones (unrelated standalones not within the above universe):

- ***Misadventures on the Night Shift*** –A hotel night shift clerk encounters her teenage fantasy: rock star Lucas Ford. And combustion ensues.

- ***Misadventures of a College Girl***—A spunky, virginal theater major meets a cocky football player at her first college party . . . and absolutely nothing goes according to plan for either of them.

- ***Misadventures on the Rebound***—A spunky woman on the rebound meets a hot, mysterious stranger in a bar on her way to her five-year high school reunion in Las Vegas and what follows is a misadventure neither of them ever imagined.

Lauren's Dark Comedy/Psych Thriller Standalone

Countdown to Killing Kurtis

A young woman with big dreams and skeletons in her closet decides her porno-king husband must die in exactly a year. This is not a traditional romance, but it will most definitely keep you turning the pages and saying "WTF?" If you're looking for something a bit outside the box, with twists and turns, suspense, and dark humor, this is the book for you: a standalone psychological thriller/dark comedy with romantic elements.

AUTHOR BIOGRAPHY

Once you enter interconnected standalone romances of USA Today and internationally bestselling author Lauren Rowe's beloved and page-turning "Rowe-verse," you'll never want to leave. Find out why readers around the globe have fallen in love with all the characters in this world, including the Faradays, the Morgans and their besties, alpha mogul Reed Rivers and the artists signed to his record label, River Records.

Be sure to explore all the incredible spoiler-free bonus materials, including original music from the books, music videos, magazine covers and interviews, plus exclusive bonus scenes, all featured on Lauren's website at www.laurenrowebooks.com

To find out about Lauren's upcoming releases and giveaways, sign up for Lauren's emails here!

Lauren loves to hear from readers! Send Lauren an email from her website, say hi on Twitter, Instagram, or Facebook.

Made in United States
Troutdale, OR
09/18/2023